THE SHROUD

Jerel Law

Cover Design: Stephen Lursen
Copyright © 2012 Jerel Law
All rights reserved.
ISBN-10: 0692295402
ISBN-13: 978-0692295403

Also by Jerel Law:

The Jonah Stone: Son of Angels series, including...

Spirit Fighter

Fire Prophet

Shadow Chaser

Truth Runner

*Thanks Dad, for always loving me,
and always loving a good book.*

Prologue

TURIN, ITALY

The team moved swiftly and silently, feet gliding over the cobblestone. The four pairs of black military boots made no sound against the cracked old brick. The street was empty, save a stray cat hurrying along in the soft moonlight.

They had left a black Humvee in the alley two blocks away from their destination, hidden in the dark shadows of an almost-empty parking lot. A large trash dumpster partially blocked the vehicle from view. The leader had scouted out the location three days ago. No detail had been left to chance.

Now, he stopped his men suddenly and, with a quick hand motion, his black-clad friends slid back against the wall. He listened. A couple emerged a block ahead of them, stumbling across the street. They laughed as the woman grabbed her partner to keep him from falling down. They kissed in the middle of the street.

The leader touched the trigger of his gun, the cold steel smooth against his finger. A handful of scenarios entered his mind, each ending with the disposal of two bodies. The men in black waited, watching. Finally, the couple moved on. The leader motioned them out to the middle of the street. They had to move fast.

In one quick movement, he pulled the manhole cover off. One by one, they silently dropped themselves below the surface of the street. He tugged the cover back in place before anyone above ground noticed. The team found an ancient set of metal stairs and descended one more level down.

A maze of old sewage tunnels stretched before them. The leader switched on a headlamp and led them forward, through the corridors. He had memorized the route from a map, in case his GPS device stopped working. Left, right, another right, another left. For now, the GPS glowed steadily, the target blinking red.

At the next intersection of tunnels, he paused, studying the display again, just to be sure.

He had made a visit to the church earlier today. Catedral di Giovannia de Baptiste. He sat patiently, listening to the ancient words uttered by an ancient priest, spoken in a deep baritone that echoed through the cavernous church. He knelt when it was appropriate, even offering a real prayer. The stained glass images glistened around him, pressing in on him until he began to rub his temples. There, with the old and the faithful, mumbling through the sacred, familiar words, his head began to throb.

After the service, he stood and moved to the center aisle. Slowly, meticulously, he paced toward the altar, his precise footsteps echoing through the silence.

He knelt again, but he did not bow. Instead, his eyes were drawn to the long, horizontal box laying face up in front of him. Such an odd-shaped item to be placed behind an altar in a cathedral. Encased in the box with a glass top was something even he had to stare at in order to believe.

A white linen shroud about fourteen feet long lay inside, spread to the edges of the box. On it was the rust-colored image of a human figure. Leaning forward, he examined it as closely as he dared. He could see the faint scars on the hands and feet. There was a mark on the side of the body, the wound from the spear. Across the brow was a smattering of marks, thought to be the scars from thorns pressed down on the victim's head.

So there it is. The famed Shroud of Turin. The burial cloth of Jesus Christ.

Of course, he knew what everyone else in the room likely knew, too. That this actually wasn't the Shroud of Turin. Not the real one. This was merely a replica, one made for viewing by the masses.

The real shroud was in the church, but hidden away among a labyrinth of rooms, in a location most people never came close to. It was only made available to the public to view every twenty-five years by the Catholic Church. The rest of its days were spent locked behind a high-tech, Israeli-made vault door. The Vatican was concerned about openly displaying the already tattered relic. Worried about mischievous kids, perhaps.

And thieves.

If my information is correct, calculated the man, *the real shroud is directly below this altar, one level down.* He knelt for what he felt was an average amount of time. Standing, he crossed himself and turned, pressing the button on the GPS device in his pocket, marking his location. Slowly, he had walked out of the church, nodding solemnly to a priest as he slid out.

He had the same black GPS locator in his hands now, in the tunnel below the church. He began to walk slowly down the tunnel to his left. Fourteen paces in, he stopped and looked up. Breaking their silence for the first time, he barked orders to the team.

"This is it. Let's make it quick."

Two floors below the sanctuary, the three men began to remove their gear. One of the men brought out a small detonator the size of a cell phone. Another carefully removed a long string of explosives, each tied to the next like a sausage link chain. Their commander was busy marking four spots with chalk on the low roof of the sewage line.

"Here, here, here, and here," he said.

The man with the explosives silently began pressing each stick against the roof, which adhered on contact. They eventually formed a rectangle directly above them.

"Ready?" said the leader. With each second that passed, he was growing more jittery and felt the urge to pull out a cigarette. They needed to get this over.

One of the men nodded, and the four backed down the tunnel. He gave the signal and, opening the detonator, the man pushed the red button. Immediately, white light filled the tunnel and a concentrated series of mini-explosions erupted, each not much louder than a Roman candle firecracker. The explosives were designed to cause just enough damage to do the job, but not enough to bring down the lower level of the church. It was a brilliant show, and within seconds the ceiling gave way. With a crash, the floor above caved in, its contents spilling onto the ground in front of them.

Smoke filled the tunnel and they had to shield their faces from the blast and the resulting dust. An alarm screamed upstairs but no one seemed to notice. As the dust lifted, all eyes were fixed on the ground.

They knelt down around the large box that had neatly dropped at their feet.

"The glass is still intact," the leader said, encouraged. He had made the correct assumption. The box had been built to withstand significant force. Reaching into his pack, he removed a glasscutter, two large suction cups, and a new pair of gloves. Attaching the black cups to either end of the glass, he carefully leaned over the shroud, cutting a line around the edges of the box. Grasping the handles of the suction cups, he lifted gently, feeling the glass give. He propped it against the rock wall.

Then he slid on a delicate pair of gloves and gently lifted the real Shroud of Turin from the box. Folding it as quickly as he dared, he placed it in the special plastic covering he had brought with him, just as he had been instructed. He sealed the plastic, creating an airtight vacuum, and stored it carefully in his backpack.

"Time to go," he said.

The men jogged down the corridors, retracing their steps. Finding the manhole cover, they climbed up the ladder, the first man pushing up the lid just enough to assess the situation. Two police cars zoomed by on a cross street a few blocks ahead. There was no one coming from either direction in their immediate vicinity.

Each man climbed up and out of the sewage line. They stayed in the shadows, blending in with the darkness. Sirens were growing louder, but none came their way. The police would no doubt congregate at the front door of the church.

The Humvee was untouched, waiting for them behind the dumpster. They drove out of the parking lot slowly, sticking to the back roads, moving further away from the sirens and the church.

For the first time that night, a smile crept onto the leader's face. He retrieved a cell phone from his bag and dialed a number. A deep voice answered.

"Well?"

The man paused, milking the excitement of the moment. This was certainly no ordinary smash and grab.

"We got it."

CHAPTER 1

One month later
Chapel Hill

I walked underneath the towering oaks on campus, taking my time. It was one of those days so perfect it makes you breathe extra deep, as if keeping that fresh air inside you a little longer might not only invigorate your body, but your soul as well. Ambling along Raleigh Street, I passed the venerated Old Well, where a student had stopped to take a friend's picture.

If time stopped also today that would be fine by me. My father once told me it's futile to look backward and frustration to try to see too far ahead, so stay in the moment and pay attention. I took that as license to enjoy this day. Besides, it finally seemed like my life was coming together. I recently got a promotion at the town newspaper as one of only two full time reporters. Which came with a decent raise. And for the first time since I graduated, five years ago, I had a steady girlfriend, a nice change from the string of short-term relationships I seem to attract.

The new brick building in front of me was styled to look old and stately, and as I approached it I tried to notice everything. Good journalists are nothing if not observant. There was a couple making out on a blanket under an oak tree. A longhaired hippie with a backpack on, throwing a Frisbee to his dog. Two girls studying on a bench beside a water fountain. A guy flying past on a mountain bike, sending a small tornado of leaves spiraling in his draft. Must be late to class.

My grandfather had been the editor of his local paper and, with my father being who he was, I guess journalism is in my blood. I don't remember ever thinking about choosing this as a career path—I just never wanted to do anything else.

I looked at my watch, breaking out of my daydream for a second. I had a deadline this afternoon that needed attention. But it could wait a little longer, at least until after I stopped in to see Daniela.

Hopping up the wide concrete steps of Hambright Hall, two at a time, I pushed through the double glass doors. Until I'd started dating Daniela, I had never set foot in the archaeology building. The journalism school was on the other side of the campus, and the last thing on my mind when I was still a student here had been digging for old stuff in the dirt.

I found lecture hall 106 and peeked through the window. Standing in front of about a hundred students was five feet and ten inches of Italian bombshell. Daniela Portonova. She had her hand perched on a hip as she lectured to the group. Her black hair fell past her shoulders. I couldn't hear what she was saying but I watched her red lips move as she spoke. I still couldn't believe this woman was going out with me.

I opened the door and strode to the back of the room. She glanced at me and paused.

"Mr. Harkin," she said, in her Italian accent, nodding to me, as she continued her lecture.

Offering her a small wave, I took a seat at the back of the class. She was speaking passionately about the latest archaeological finds in northern Jerusalem. Some people are fascinated endlessly by the digs that uncover ancient, rust-eaten coins and cups from eras past. I am not one of them. At least the scenery isn't boring, I told myself as I watched her move around the classroom.

I had dropped in on her a couple of times, earlier in the semester. Just to listen to her speak with that incredible accent. We had met in the dead of winter at a high-dollar fundraiser we both were required to attend. She, because she was the new superstar professor of the vaunted archaeology department, and me, because I had to cover another less-than-exciting story for the paper. I'd found her at a quiet table in the bar, hiding behind a drink and her phone, having escaped the loudmouthed donors and glad-handing politicians. It had taken awhile to crack through the steely façade of disinterest she projected, but after a barrage of the cheesiest one-liners I could come up with, she finally smiled. And one smile was all the encouragement I needed. She agreed to see me the next night.

As I listened to her lecture now, I quickly realized she was a bit off. Something wasn't quite right. As I said, observation is one of my strong suits and today, she seemed distracted. I counted five times in ten minutes that she looked at her watch. Once she even dropped her notes on the floor. Twice she stopped in mid-sentence, forgetting where she was, apologizing to the class.

Even distracted, though, she was still excited about her archaeology. You could tell when she gave in to her passion, because her voice grew higher and her words came out at a faster clip. There was a different lilt to it. Her glasses kept sliding down her nose and she kept having to push them back into place. The faster she talked, the quicker they slid.

When she ended class early, the students glanced at each other in surprise, then wasted no time, grabbing their bags and making for the door.

"That's a first," a guy in a baseball cap muttered as he passed me. "But no complaints here."

I waited in my seat until most of the students were gone and then walked to the front, where Daniela was scurrying around, grabbing stray papers and books and shoving them into her leather satchel.

"Hey there," I said, smiling.

She looked up, offering me a rushed smile. "Matthew," she said, "why did you come into my class so late?"

"I know, I do apologize for that. I was in the gym for my usual three-hour workout and got a little carried away with the bench press," I smiled, stretching my muscles. "The football team needed some help…"

"Hmm," she said, grabbing my right arm. "I don't think you stayed long enough."

"Ouch, professor," I said, pulling my arm back. "Low blow."

She leveled her serious, I'm-done-kidding-with-you gaze at me. "I believe I am ready to do that interview you've been asking about."

I folded my arms. I'd asked her twice during my first date to grant me an interview. I thought it would be a good human interest piece, a world-renowned Italian professor landing at our school after what amounted to a bidding war with two Ivy League schools. At least, that's what I'd been able to discover from other sources. There was a good story there. Let's just say, though, I had a little human interest of my own happening here. She had stonewalled me, though, and I had stopped bugging her about it.

"Are you sure?"

"Tonight, seven o'clock," she said, throwing her bag over her shoulder.

"Okay," I said. "How about 411 West, downtown? I'll pick you up."

She smiled. "Let's meet there, shall we?"

And with that, she brushed by me and was gone. Catching her perfume wafting upward, I was reminded of the honeysuckle covering my backyard where I grew up.

I couldn't help but smile as I watched her leave.

CHAPTER 2

I like to ask questions. Being a reporter is second nature to me—it's almost an involuntary muscle movement, like breathing. Questions are the language my brain speaks. Answers are what any journalist worth anything wants, but I've already learned that real answers are hard to come by. Every question leads to an answer which brings on another question, with yet another answer. And by the way, most answers aren't really answers. This is what they taught us in journalism school. It's also what my father preached. Most answers are smokescreens, veils to peer through, leading to more questions. It's like digging for lost treasure. Every shovel full of dirt leads you deeper, closer to what you hope is the truth. But it can be a painstaking process.

I'm good with questions. Answers . . . well, those are usually in shorter supply.

I came armed with questions for Daniela. I met her at the front of the small, Italian restaurant, and she gave me a soft embrace. I realized at the last second I had suggested an American Italian place to a real Italian. I smacked myself on the forehead as I followed her inside.

"A table in the corner, please," she asked the hostess. I wanted a table in the middle of everything, so everyone could see me with the beautiful professor. But I wasn't about to push it.

We sat down and I ordered a bottle of wine.

"This is an interview, not a date," she said. She was toying with me.

"Should I recall that wine then? Waitress?" I called out loudly, raising my hand.

Daniela pulled my hand down to the table and cut her eyes around the restaurant. "Don't be ridiculous, Matthew. You're going to disturb people."

Shrugging my shoulders, I winked at her. "Guess we'll keep the wine then."

I flipped through the notebook sitting on the table in front of me. "I need to warn you," I said, "I can be a hard interviewer. I know we're dating and everything, but I won't hold back. I've been known to make people break down and cry. You may want to have some Kleenex handy. Have you ever seen Oprah Winfrey do an interview? She's got nothing on me."

"I'm not afraid. Let's get started."

She smiled, her hazel eyes dancing. Her hair was down and when our eyes met I melted a little inside. I swallowed, glancing away for a second, and then brought out a tape recorder and placed it in the center of the table. She raised her eyebrows, but didn't refuse.

"Alright, Professor Portonova, tell me about yourself, then, and the story of how you made your way into God's country."

The hazel eyes stared at me. "God's…?"

"I'm sorry," I said. "I mean, Chapel Hill."

She rolled her eyes. "Yes, of course, how could I forget? How about calling it basketball country? It's all you people talk about around here. Even the other professors. They can't miss a game."

"Well, it is God's favorite sport. There's little doubt about that. And you know what color the sky is, don't you?"

"Yes, yes, Carolina blue. I get it," she dismissed the conversation with a wave of her hand. "But back to your question. I grew up in Torino, Italy."

"Torino? As in, Turin? Weren't the winter Olympics there a while back?"

"Yes, they were," she said, sitting up, a hint of pride in her voice. "The world finally was able to see how beautiful my hometown is."

11

"I remember watching some of it on television," I said. "You're right, it was beautiful. The mountains were amazing."

She beamed. "You can see snow on the Alps all year long. It is unlike anywhere around here. I miss it very much."

"Is your family still there?"

"My father is, yes. My mother passed away five years ago," she added, quietly. "I have a sister in Florence, studying art."

"Oh," I said, frowning. "I'm sorry, I didn't know that."

I could tell from how she paused that the memory of her mother's death was fresh. I wasn't going to press her. The waitress brought the wine, and we waited as she poured our glasses.

"I studied at the university in Rome," she continued, signaling that the topic of her family was finished. "A double-major in archaeology and ancient near eastern history, with a minor in chemistry."

"So you had a great social life in Rome, then?" I asked. She cocked her head to the side and stared. "Sorry, I forget you don't get American sarcasm."

"I was very busy there. Not enough time for things like…this." She took a sip of wine and spent a moment glancing around the room. "Anyway, when I graduated the PhD program in Rome, they immediately offered me an associate professorship, which I took. I did a lot of research, wrote a few journal articles, and voila, here I am, at arguably the best school for archaeology in the country."

"From what I understand, it is the best, now that you're here." It sounded like I was sucking up to her, but really, I wasn't. I'd done my research on the good professor, and apparently she was one of the top three up-and-coming archaeology experts. Not just in the United States. In the world. She had authored two books widely regarded as the top in their category, and co-authored at least thirteen textbooks. She was underselling herself. One more reason I liked her.

And here she was, dating me. A regular Joe from North Carolina. Go figure.

"Matthew, don't believe everything you read online. That's not a good habit for a journalist to develop," she said sweetly, taking another sip from her glass. "And please don't call me 'professor.'"

"It's for interview purposes, Professor," I replied. I held up the recorder directly in front of her. "So are you dating anyone? For the official record, of course."

"No comment," she said, leaning back in her chair as she held her glass aloft.

I cocked my head sideways. "That's not what I hear."

She grabbed the recorder from my hand and placed it back on the table. "So tell me about you, Matthew."

"You're going to interview me now?" I asked. "Well, I guess that's fair. The answers are not going to be very exciting, though. I've told you some of this already. I grew up in Eastern North Carolina and lived the typical Southern boy childhood. Which means I played in the woods a lot, built tree forts, and tipped some cows. The usual. Then when I was ten, my father moved us to Manhattan, where I lived until college."

"What about your family?" she asked. "Do you miss them?"

I considered how to answer that one. Like I said, I'm better at questions than answers. "I miss my mother and my sister." I took another sip of wine, trying to decide if I should let this particular cat out of the bag. I hadn't yet, not with her. "And my father too. But he passed away about this time last year."

"Oh," she said, with a look of genuine concern. "I'm so sorry." I could tell she wasn't sure how to respond. "You don't have to talk about it if you don't want to."

It's not the most comfortable story to tell. The memories are raw, even though I've done a good job of stuffing them down a long passageway in my heart. But for her, I would try.

"He was a reporter for CNN, and got into a hostage situation in Iraq. He was on video, in some dark, dirty room, surrounded by people with masks and guns, making threats and demands. It was broadcast by Al-Jazeera, you know, the whole nine yards. As you probably are aware, 'The U.S. government doesn't negotiate with terrorists,' so the terrorists decided to make an example of him. They did it right there on live international television."

I waited for the light bulb to come on.

"Wait. Your father was…"

"Buddy Harkin. Yep, the one and only."

Even before his death, he was mentioned in the same breath with Brokaw, Blitzer, Anderson Cooper, and even Geraldo Rivera every once in awhile, which always made my stomach turn. Since he was killed, though, his reputation had soared through the roof, into almost household-name status.

She reached over and took my hand. "I remember the stories. It was everywhere. Shocking, what happened. I remember seeing his face on the news. Matthew, I had no idea…you didn't tell me…"

I put my hand up. "It's okay. I've dealt with it in my own way. I'm good." I softly patted her on top of her hand and smiled broadly. I could tell she didn't believe me, but at least she didn't say it. My father was in so many ways my hero. I wanted everything to be okay, but the reality was I had barely been able to cope with it.

Thankfully, our food arrived. Chicken and pasta for her, shrimp and grits for me. We ate in silence for a while. I stole glances at her. It didn't take an all-star journalist to realize she was growing nervous again. My thoughts ran back to her state of being in her classroom earlier. Something was on her mind besides this conversation, and I wondered if I would find out what it was by night's end.

She looked up from her pasta and, like she'd finally made up her mind about something, said, "Did you hear about the shroud?"

I chewed on a bite of shrimp, drawing a blank until it dawned on me. "Do you mean the Shroud of Turin? The burial cloth of Jesus himself?"

She nodded.

I cycled through what I knew about the shroud. It wasn't a lot. "I've heard of it, if that's what you mean. Fanatics think it's the cloth that was actually wrapped around Jesus after he was crucified. It's supposed to have an image of Christ on it, right?" Something I had read earlier suddenly came to mind. "You did your doctoral thesis on the shroud, didn't you?"

Her eyes sparkled, but she was cautious. "Correct. Growing up in Turin, it was always fascinating to me. It is a fourteen-foot long section of linen, with a brown image that appears to be the imprint of a man who was crucified."

I raised my glass, swirling the wine around a bit. "One more theory for the zealots to believe. Whoever faked it should have sold tickets. The religious wackos love stuff like that. As a matter of fact, I saw on eBay where you can buy a toaster that prints a perfect picture of Jesus on top of your grilled cheese sandwich. It's called the Grilled Cheesus."

She laughed, in spite of her attempts to keep herself from reacting.

"It's true," I pressed. "I'll have one sent over."

She drew her face tight again. "One month ago, the Shroud of Turin was stolen out of the Catedral di Giovannia de Baptiste. The Cathedral of Saint John the Baptist."

"Hmmm," I said, taking another bite. "Someone couldn't wait to have it in their collection."

"Perhaps."

15

I studied her face. She would make a good poker player. Difficult to read. "It is a fake, right? From what I recall, most of the scientific community thinks so. Only a few radicals out there actually believe the Shroud of Turin is the real deal. My question, Professor Portonova, is what do you believe?"

She cleared her throat. "Many brilliant people have written it off as false, a piece of Middle Age religious propaganda. They have hypothesized it was painted by an ingenious scam artist. Or that it was actually a primitive photograph, by none other than Leonardo da Vinci himself."

I interrupted her. "Da Vinci, huh? That's fascinating. But I want to hear what you think, Daniela."

Her voice softened as she toyed with her pasta. "I do not believe the shroud is a forgery."

I sat back in my chair. This was a strange turn in the conversation but I was intrigued. "So you think this is the actual cloth they wrapped around Jesus Christ himself? That we have a real, historical item that was touching the body of Christ? That this isn't a bunch of voodoo mythology the church cooked up?"

My question didn't phase her.

"That is the only conclusion we have left."

CHAPTER 3

I could tell she was trying to decide what she wanted to say, and how to say it. I'd never seen her be so careful with her words. My father used to say that, in an interview, expect people to tell you about ten percent of what they know, if that. The rest of the truth is in there, but it takes a good question, sometimes even a little bullying, to get to the truth. Other times, it just takes waiting.

The funny thing is, I could still hear him say, *most people, even people who have done really bad things, will trip all over themselves to tell you the truth. They want to do it.*

I chose to wait.

"What I am saying, Matthew," she said, pushing her hair behind her ears, "is that the shroud is not a forgery. Many, many people throughout history have believed it was. In fact, as recently as 1989, research was done that apparently proved the fabric dated to the Middle Ages. It was written off as some kind of grand, genius hoax, or an elaborate tribute of faith in Christ. As I said, some even suggested da Vinci was the creator of the image."

"That makes some sense," I said. "If I remember my medieval history right, there were lots of religious relics floating around at that time. And folks could buy one. Fakes, designed to entice the poor and make somebody a buck or two in the process."

"Yes, that happened quite often," Daniela nodded. "So the Shroud of Turin was written off as just such an artifact. Until a few years ago. More research was conducted on the fibers of the shroud and it was determined the test samples they used in 1989 were in fact from a section of the cloth that had been repaired."

I shrugged. "What does that mean?"

"Well, this is where it gets even more interesting," she said. "The church the shroud was housed in burned to the ground in 1532. The cloth was protected from many things—in fact, it was sealed in a metal box. But as the

17

heat got to it, part of the box melted, dripping hot metal onto the corner of the shroud. There were certain segments of damaged cloth that were craftily replaced by a group of nuns."

"Ah yes, the Seven Sewing Nuns of the Shroud. My mom used to read me that story at bedtime." I snorted. I can't believe the depths of my own sarcasm sometimes. I just can't help myself. She didn't find this as amusing as I did.

"Anyway," she continued, "the shroud was examined by Maggie Duncan, a world-renowned textiles expert. You must understand, the Roman Catholic Church guards the Shroud of Turin as if their very existence depends on it. Not many people have ever touched it. But she was allowed to study it, and when she did, she discovered there were sewn patches that dated to the 1500s. This clearly indicated repairs had been made. But she noticed something else that was shocking in the scientific and archaeological communities. The pattern of the weaving of the linen, and the material itself, is of a consistency that dates it much, much earlier."

"How much earlier?" She had me. Despite my penchant for sarcasm, I was growing genuinely interested in this story.

"To the first century," she said, and with that declaration, she took a bite of linguini.

"That's interesting," I said. "It really is. You have me intrigued. But Daniela, that doesn't really prove anything. So what? We have a piece of old cloth from the first century. Big deal. It has an image of a guy who apparently was crucified. It could still have been painted on by some first century artist."

"That is correct," she said, pointing her fork at me. "It could have been. Except for the fact that no self-respecting scientist, after studying the evidence, honestly believes that what is on that piece of linen cloth is paint."

"What is it then? Blood?"

"No," she said.

"Dirt?"

She stared at me like a knowledgeable professor to an uninformed student. "It's not dirt."

"Well, you're the professor, and I give up. You tell me what it is."

She took a sip of wine. "At the turn of the twentieth century a photographer was allowed unparalleled access to the shroud. He took the first pictures. And an unexpected thing happened when he was in the darkroom. He developed the photographs, and realized his negative actually contained the clear, unmistakable image of the man crucified. It was uncanny how much this image looked like a real human being who had been scourged, beaten, and nailed to a wooden beam."

I felt a fog of confusion setting in. "You mean, in the darkroom he realizes that his negative actually looks like a real picture of the guy?"

She nods, waiting for me to put it together.

"So the real image of the shroud is a…"

"It is a photographic negative."

I swallowed another bite of food, chewing slowly as I thought this through. "How is that possible?"

"No one can say for sure," she said. "Scientists and scholars debate it all the time. How does a perfect negative image show up on a first-century cloth? How could that happen? No one knows, no one has an answer. So some brush it aside. Others grope for answers. The problem then is that we enter the realm of speculation and leave science behind—in the dust, I believe you Americans say?"

She is very cute when she says that with her Italian accent. I smiled. "Yes, in the dust." We lock eyes.

"So, Professor," I said. "What do you do with all of that?"

She makes a sweeping motion with her arm. "I think I brush it aside." She attempts to laugh, but it comes out sounding hollow. I press her for more.

"How close have you, personally, been to the shroud? Have you ever touched it?"

She glanced at me and then quickly looked away, her eyes darting around the room again. Her next sentence was carefully worded, and she leaned in over the recorder to say it. "I have had an opportunity to study the Shroud of Turin closely."

"Really? I mean, for someone like you, that had to be a thrill, right? You wrote your doctoral thesis on it, for goodness sake."

"What can I say? It was an overwhelming experience." She sat back in her chair and crossed her legs, looking at me with a kind of finality that told me this was the end of that line of questioning.

They will bend a lot, dad would say, *but you don't want to see them break. It's not good for you, them, or your story.*

But I was interested in this thing now, in spite of myself, and the questions wouldn't stop rolling around in my head. My dad and I had our differences but this is where we are exactly alike. Where there is smoke, there is bound to be some fire. And apparently the men in my family tend to be the guys who like to get up close and watch things burn.

Daniela was flustered. Even more than she had been earlier. "Let's get out of here," she said, grabbing her purse. "I need to run to the ladies' room, though. Meet me out front?"

Our plates were still half full, but I nodded, paid the bill and waited for her beneath the neon restaurant sign. The shrimp and grits were sitting well with the wine, and I breathed in the crisp night air, trying to sort out the conversation. Classifying it into knowns and unknowns, answers and questions. Which led to more questions. As usual.

She emerged, locked her arm in mine, and quickly ushered me around the corner. She glanced behind us twice.

"Are you in hurry or something?" I joked.

She frowned. "Just a little cold. That's all."

We walked together in silence to her car. She held my hand lightly, and walked close to me. Suddenly she seemed very vulnerable, and alone. Not the confident Professor Portonova I had seen in her classroom earlier, that Italian beauty I had noticed at that fundraiser a few months ago. Right now, she just seemed afraid.

"Let me ask you one more thing," I said, turning toward her in the darkness of the parking lot. "Who in their right mind would steal the shroud? I get it, it's an important relic and we should protect and cherish it. But it's history. Why would anyone go to the effort to take it? Especially if it is as well-guarded as you described."

Maybe it was the shadows the street lamp cast across her face, but she seemed to grow two shades darker. "There are people out there who believe the shroud is more than just a historical relic, Matthew. There are some who believe it can point to even more important and significant artifacts. And locations."

"Such as?"

She sighed. I was really pressing my luck, but something was driving her to tell me. I could tell she wanted to. And then she grasped my arm and drew me close to her, putting her lips beside my ear. "A place that, if found, would literally change the world as we know it. That would lead some to commit crimes, even murder, in order to keep the location hidden."

What did that mean? She had to be exaggerating. But she seemed deadly serious...I could tell she really believed it.

"What people?" I asked.

She rubbed her arms, shaking her head. "People in very powerful, very influential positions. With a lot of money, a lot of sway. I've seen what they can do."

My mind swirled. "But what place are you talking about? I don't understand. What is this place that's so important it would change the world, like you say?"

She sighed, her voice barely above a whisper. "The tomb of Jesus himself."

I blinked for a few seconds, my mind spinning into overdrive. "But…"

"Enough," she interrupted. Grabbing the back of my head, she guided my face down to hers. I didn't fight it. Her full lips tasted sweet as we kissed in the moonlight. I didn't notice that her left hand slid into my jacket pocket.

"I have to go," she said abruptly. She turned to me and our eyes met again. "Thanks for the interview. It wasn't so bad after all." She flashed a quick smile, and then added, "And I am truly sorry about your father."

"Hey!" I called out after her. "Wait…what's the rush?"

She didn't turn back around. Jumping into her convertible, she backed out, waved to me, and sped away.

Leaving me once again with more questions than answers.

CHAPTER 4

I was glad she left first in her candy red Audi. That way she wouldn't have to see me leave in my 1996 Honda Accord, with 232,000 miles on it. She'd seen it before, but it was one more reminder I didn't need of the fact that I was dating someone way out of my league.

The truth was, I was somewhat broke, and what little money I had left after my mortgage and other bills usually found its way to He's Not Here, the local bar. Besides, I had access to a nicer ride when I wanted it, courtesy of my roommate. He just happened to need it tonight.

I drove slowly through the tree-lined streets of an old neighborhood. It was quiet and I took it slowly, windows rolled down. I had a lot on my mind, much more to digest tonight than the shrimp and grits.

I hadn't spoken about my father in almost a year. After tonight, I couldn't help but see his face. He always seemed to be on the edge of something important, dangerous, and intense. He would come and visit for a week or so every couple of months, bringing strange and wonderful gifts from all over the world. Middle eastern relics, African artwork that hung on our walls, a sherpa's walking staff from Nepal. He was loud, boisterous, and fun. My memories of him mostly are of him wearing a smirking smile on his face. And stays that never lasted long enough. Too soon, he would kiss my mother, and be off again.

They had a strange relationship, my mom and dad. When he would come around, her eyes would light up. But I would also hear fighting in their bedroom. Mom wanted him to quit, or take a desk job. Something safe, where he would be closer to the family, closer to her. He didn't understand, said she was crazy, that he would never do it. *Look at our apartment in Manhattan, the things we can buy, the lifestyle, the notoriety we have.* His job gave us that, he would

23

say. Deep down, I think she was happy for his success, but at the same time despising the job that took him away from his son and daughter. She was angry with him for letting it happen.

I didn't see him for half of my childhood. I guess I should have been mad about that. Instead, I just missed him terribly, then and now. I wasn't sure I would become half the reporter he ever was.

I pulled into the driveway of my recently purchased, ancient two-story house, parking under the canopy created by a couple of huge old oaks. I heard the shouting before I made it to the porch. I let the screen door slam shut on the way in, threw my keys on the counter, and realized Hoffman was on the phone, yelling. I didn't have to guess who was on the other end of the line.

"Dad, I don't need you to tell me what to—" He stopped, listening, pacing down the small hallway, into and out of the den.

"I understand, but you're not listening ei—"

I could hear his father's voice blaring through the phone. I walked in, waved at him with a big, fake smile, hoping to lighten the mood, but he was too caught up to see me.

My dad used to call my roommate, Hoffman Schwaab, a piece of work. The son of a hedge fund manager from the rich side of Connecticut, he managed to skate through life, avoiding responsibility along the way. Loud, overweight, and already balding on top, he was the life of the party. He was the party. His dad had always been there to bail him out.

Two months ago, Hoffman was at a bar with some friends, had a few too many, and decided to drive his silver Jeep back home anyway. The cop pulled him over driving down the opposite side of Franklin Street, right through the middle of town.

"Do you know who my father is?" Hoffman yelled at the officer, laughing. "Let me tell you, he's best friends with the governor in this state of yours. They went on a fishing trip together just last month. So you might as well just let me go now."

None of this sat well with the officer, who subsequently arrested him and made a big show of it. Cuffs, flashing lights, a pat down in the middle of the street with dozens of onlookers, all the while Hoffman screaming at him.

Two hours later, Hoffman was back at our house, laughing about it.

"Just a quick phone call, that's all," he'd said.

"You go to hell!" Hoffman yelled, and then, silence. Until I heard the phone hit the wall.

Hoff and I are two very different people. You put us in the real world together, and we'd probably never hang out, never get to know each other. We met in college, though, and became tight friends. It's amazing what happens through the random system of dormitory placement. He lived across the hall from me during our freshman year and we clicked.

Our junior year his father had had enough. Enough of the partying, terrible grades, and wasting his money. He wanted to pull Hoffman out of school, bring him back home. I couldn't blame him – if it were my kid I would have done the same thing. But Hoff and I had become friends, and I stood up for him with his father, somehow convincing him to give his son another chance. After that, I pulled him through more than one class he was failing with late-night study sessions. I don't know how many parties I dragged him out of that year, so he could prepare for a test or write a paper due the next day.

Hoff plopped down in the plaid easy chair and began talking out loud to no one in particular. I left him alone and made my way up the stairs, toward my room. On the way, I knocked lightly on another door.

"Dah," a Russian voice responded.

I pushed open the door. "What's up, Pasha?"

Our other roommate, Pasha Griecko, was sitting way too close to a ridiculously large computer monitor. He pushed his thick glasses back up his nose but it wasn't as endearing on him as it was on Daniela. He didn't look at me. "It is good."

He was typing some kind of computer code indecipherable to most of the human population. His fingers moved at light speed, the cursor screaming back and forth across the high-definition screen. Books were stacked around the room, some open, others closed, a few thrown on the floor. His room was a full-fledged disaster area. Papers, dirty clothes, and pink cans of Tab were littered everywhere.

He continued glaring at the screen as he popped open a fresh can.

"Pasha, where do you get this stuff?" I asked, holding up the can. "This has to be the worst soft drink ever made. I thought people stopped drinking it in the eighties."

"Phil's Kwik-E-Mart," he said proudly. "I buy entire selection. It is the first American drink ever I taste in Kazakhstan. I love it."

"I'm sorry that was your first American experience with carbonated beverages," I said, clearing a stack of newspapers off the brownish love seat in the corner and taking a seat. "You could have at least had a diet Coke or something."

To understand Pasha, first of all you need to know he is undeniably brilliant. He had attended the university on full scholarship, due to the fact that he won a major chess tournament in Europe. I'm not a chess player, but I know he beat the guy who beat Big Blue, the chess-playing super-computer. And that guy hadn't lost in twenty-three years. Pasha took him to the Russian cleaners when he was sixteen.

He grew up in a coal mining city in Kazakhstan you've never heard of. A smart kid living in a city where no one left home because there was nothing to leave home for. In a place where it wasn't uncommon for eleven-year-olds to become alcoholics, he instead began playing chess with old men in the town square. His home life was a wreck, which I'd come to learn along the way, though he spoke of it sparingly. His father would come in and out of their lives, often violent and drunk.

"I never knew if he would greet me with a gift or a slap in the face," he'd told me once.

Pasha showed an aptitude for chess and several men took him under their wing, tutoring him, and eventually entering him into tournaments to compete, sending him on long train rides away from home, alone, at a very young age. He began to win almost every time.

At a big, continent-wide tournament, a regent of the University of North Carolina noticed him. He was one of those kids who could help make the school a more well-rounded place.

One thing led to another, and Pasha Griecko was given an American sponsor, and a full ride to a great university. We ran into each other—literally—one day on the way to class. I was late, as usual, and he was coming around the corner buried in a computer science book. We collided and my laptop bag went flying, spilling the computer onto the brick sidewalk.

When I picked up my laptop, I realized the monitor was almost fully detached from the keyboard. "Oh man," I said. "All my stuff is in here! My articles, my homework, papers…everything."

Pasha looked from me, to the shattered computer, and back to me. "You back up, yes?"

"Uh, not exactly," I said, shrugging my shoulders. "Details, you know. Not exactly my strong suit."

"You Americans, always in a hurry," he frowned. "Come with me. I fix for you."

I hesitated, pointing in the other direction. "I need to get to class."

"Without laptop?"

Good point. "You can fix this? What are you, some kind of computer genius?" I chuckled.

He looked at me and extended his hand, apparently not sensing the sarcasm. "Yes. I am Pasha Griecko, from Kazakhstan. Come. I fix computer."

We went to his cramped dorm room on the other side of campus. In about five minutes, he had my laptop spread out on his desk, fully disassembled.

I didn't want to be impolite, but we weren't exactly at a high-tech computer shop. And I had almost two thousand dollars worth of metal spread out in some Russian guy's dorm room. "Are you sure you know what you're doing?"

"Almost finished," he replied. And sure enough, a few minutes later, he had it back together. "Here. It is working now."

"Sweet," I said, as he handed it back to me. I looked it over carefully. "Thanks. I totally owe you."

He nodded, smiling shyly.

I kept running into him that semester. He was always alone, and I began to think about how it must be pretty lonely for him so far from home. I'm no saint or anything...just trying to put myself in someone else's shoes.

So when Hoff and I decided to get this house together and needed a third roommate, I lobbied hard for Pasha. At least between Hoffman Schwaab and Pasha Griecko, life around the house was never be dull.

"What are you working on?" I said, as I sprawled out in the chair.

"Java network application programming interface," Pasha said, as if he were reading the alphabet. To me, he may as well have been speaking Russian.

"Ok," I responded, brilliantly.

Pasha hit Enter, and turned with his crooked grin. "Hoff said you went on date. With professor again."

"Strictly professional," I said, though I couldn't help but smile. "For an interview."

"Of course, of course, an interview," he said. "Did she *reveal* anything interesting to you?" He laughed loudly at himself.

I smirked. "Funny Russian make big joke."

"Well, I thought it was pretty funny," Hoffman said, standing in the doorway. "Did she give you a big scoop?"

Pasha and Hoff thought this was hilariously funny. They both roared.

"Maybe she give him some new instruction," offered Pasha. They hooted again.

"Some special tutoring," Hoff added.

I just looked at them and kept smiling. I was going to let them have their fun. I had been pretty tight-lipped about my relationship with Daniela, and they weren't getting anything out of me about her. Not tonight.

"Okay, boys, settle down," I said. "Not much to report from my night with the professor. We had a nice dinner, we talked, I interviewed her for an article. We drank some good wine. That's about it."

"That's about it?" Hoff said, clearly disappointed. "Haven't you seen her more than twice now? Aren't you guys dating at this point?"

I hesitated too long.

That was all the time Hoff needed to draw his conclusion. "Matt's dating the professor!"

Suddenly he rushed over to Pasha in mock celebration, grabbing him with two hands by his shirt collar.

"Matt's dating the professor!" Hoff shouted again, in Pasha's face. "Matt's dating the professor!"

Pasha looked at him as if he'd just stepped off the edge of sanity. But Hoffman's enthusiasm could be difficult to resist. Soon the Russian broke into a goofy half grin, and gave me two thumbs up.

I watched them for a few seconds. "You guys need to grow up," I said.

"This calls for something. A celebration!" Hoffman announced. The man with the plan, he always had something cooking. "Let's go to Four Corners."

Pasha was enthralled now and had forgotten about his computer work. "Dah! Four Corners!"

"Seriously, guys?" I managed, half-heartedly. Four Corners was a college dive bar in the heart of Chapel Hill. But I really had to get working on my article. "Aren't we a little old for that?"

But there were days where we longed to be college kids again. And if we couldn't be actual students any more, we could at least act like them every once in awhile. Plus, Hoff and Pasha suddenly looked like eager puppies.

I sighed. "Okay, okay. Give me a few minutes here."

They gave each other a high-five and walked out of the room.

I set my phone on the dresser in my room when I heard it buzz. Picking it up again, I saw a new text from Daniela.

> *Matt, I'm scared. I think someone's in my apartment.*

My brow wrinkled as I typed her back quickly.

> *Who? Are you ok? Do you want me to come over?*

I stared at the phone, as a slow minute passed.

> *Yes, please!*

I replied as I hurried through our den.

> *I'll be right there, don't worry, ok?*

CHAPTER 5

I fidgeted with my cell phone as Hoffman wheeled out of our house and threw his jeep into gear. Hoff and Pasha insisted on coming with me after I told them about the text. I sent her a few more messages in the car. Each time I didn't get a response, though, and I felt my heart rate increasing.

"Can we go a little faster, Hoff?" I growled, even though he was gunning it at every opportunity.

"I'm giving it all I have here, Mattie," he said. "We'll get there soon. Besides, I'm sure she's fine. Maybe she'll want to join us at Four Corners. Sounds like she may need a drink anyway."

I shrugged. "Maybe so."

Hoffman gunned it around a curve and sent Pasha sprawling across the back seat, slamming into the side of the car.

"Slow down, idiot! You want to get us killed?" Pasha griped. I said nothing, holding on tight and looking straight ahead.

Hoff slammed the breaks at the very last second, which slid the Jeep sideways.

That was enough for me. "Okay, Hoff," I said, trying to play it cool. "You're scaring the Russian."

"I am Kazakh, not Russian!" Pasha yelled, as we slid around another turn.

Mercifully, Hoffman slowed the Jeep as we came up to Daniela's apartment complex and looked for a place to park. The lot was full.

"Just leave it here," I said, pointing to a place right behind two other cars. "We won't be here long anyway."

I hopped out as the jeep was rolling to a stop. Looking up as I walked through the parking lot, I searched for her third-floor apartment balcony.

"Come on, guys," I called back to them. "Keep up."

I spotted it, with lights on in the living room, and was about to hustle up the steps below when movement caught my attention. I stopped in my tracks.

Pasha and Hoffman looked upward too, and saw what I did – two people standing in the living room, the sliding glass door shut.

One of them was Daniela.

The other was a man holding a gun above his head.

They were arguing, and I saw him grip her arm in his hand. Everything began to happen in slow motion. I wanted to run inside, up the steps. But my feet were frozen.

"Daniela!" I cried out.

She tore away from him and slammed herself into the glass door, so hard that I couldn't believe it didn't break. Forcing it open, she backed out onto the balcony.

The man, tall and thin, with platinum blond hair, followed her quickly. He slapped one hand over her mouth, holding the gun to her forehead in the other.

Yanking her up straight, without hesitation, he pulled the trigger twice. I heard two pops, muffled, but deadly forceful.

We stood in horror as her body tumbled through the air for two eternal seconds of silence, broken by the impact of her body falling into the bushes below.

The man stared down for a long time. And then he saw us. His eyes narrowed, holding our gaze for a few seconds, and then he ran back inside.

Somehow that freed my feet to move again, and I ran toward her.

"I'm calling the police!" Hoffman said, trying to still his shaking hand.

"Oh my God," Pasha was saying, over and over again. I vaguely noticed him crossing himself above his chest with a trembling hand as we ran over. I couldn't think. I reached her body first. *Maybe somehow she's still alive, by some kind of miracle.*

Her body was laying facedown. The back of her head was shredded by the two bullets shot at close range. I pulled her off of the bushes and lifted her gently down to the ground. A strange feeling swept through me as my fingers touched the skin of her ankle.

"The police are on the way," Hoffman said as he ran over, breathing heavily. He was glancing all around. "Do you think he's coming after us?"

In that moment I didn't care if he did. Within seconds, the police sirens were blaring.

"Should we…be touching her, Matt?" Pasha asked.

I ignored him, turning her slowly over in my trembling hands, so that I was close to her face.

"Jesus…" I whispered, as I saw her face. "Oh, no, no, no…".

I touched her hairline with my finger, just above where the two bullets had entered. Her vacant eyes terrified me, but I couldn't look away.

We stood over her in silence until the police cruisers screeched into the parking lot.

CHAPTER 6

The next several hours were a blur, a flurry of people and sirens and police detectives and questions. I told the story a dozen different times to a dozen different people, who all wanted to hear the same things over and over again. I was a reporter, so on one hand I could understand the process, but this was ridiculous. The main detective was a guy named Detective Donnelly. We were in a room that smelled like my high school locker room. Sweat and adrenaline. Donnelly came in and out, in and out. I was alone, and the others, I assumed, were in separate rooms just like mine, but they wouldn't tell me. They were trying to establish our innocence—or our guilt. Did our stories corroborate? Were we saying the same things?

So the questions kept coming. *What did you see? Why were you there? Where were you earlier tonight?* Of course, when I told them I had dinner with her and that we'd been dating some, the questions came faster. *When did you meet her? How long have you been serious? What did she say to you tonight? Was she suspicious of anyone?* And on and on.

I recounted as much of our dinner conversation as I could remember. They wanted all the facts, like that I had the shrimp and grits and she had pasta. I was numb but, as that began to wear off, I found myself growing angry. I wanted them to catch whoever did it, and I would do whatever I could to help. I realized answering them as clearly as possible could only move this along. I'm good at remembering details, so I told them everything. The date of the bottle of wine, the price of the check.

Someone killed Daniela. I still couldn't believe it. It was surreal. But it had happened.

"So you got a good look at this guy's face?" Donnelly burst in, placing both hands on the table and staring down at me.

"I've said this a few times already, haven't I?" I said. I was beginning to feel chippy. I didn't care how I sounded any more. "I've described it as well as I can. Shouldn't you be out looking for this guy right now instead of asking me the same questions over and over again?"

He put his crooked finger in my face. "It's in your best interest to answer questions as many times as I want you to."

I had seen him, albeit very briefly. He stood over her in the living room, then on the balcony. In slow motion, over and over again, the scene replayed in my mind.

"I told you, he was tall, thin, wearing a trench coat or long jacket, that he had bleached blond hair, short cut..."

I felt the first wave of emotion come up from my gut and lodge in my throat. Donnelly sensed it, sighed, and some of the tension in the room eased. He walked out of the room again.

The police seemed to suspect armed robbery and possible sexual assault, pending their examination of the body. A thug spies her, considers her an easy target, follows her for a while, and finally makes his move.

Even though I was no detective, something about that didn't sit well with me. *Maybe you just don't want it to be true,* I told myself.

At three o'clock in the morning, I finally got to see Hoffman and Pasha. They looked weary, just like I was sure I did. Four hours straight of intense questioning had definitely taken its toll. And we were simply witnesses.

"Jeez, imagine if we were suspects?" I wondered out loud.

They let us go home together, which I took to be a good sign. Detective Donnelly said he would be in touch, to not stray too far away, and that they still might need our help. Each of us left with his card in our back pockets. He saw us out to the parking lot, where a police officer had parked Hoff's Jeep.

"Have either of you seen anybody die before?" Hoffman finally said, interrupting the silent ride home. We were exhausted and still in shock, but both Pasha and I shook our heads. In spite of what they say about violent acts on television and how they desensitize you to real violence, nothing had prepared me for the real thing. Seeing thousands and thousands of people killed in the movies was nothing like witnessing it in person.

I couldn't get the sensations of it out of my head. The sound of a body hitting the bushes. The smell of blood mixed with burnt flesh from a close gunshot wound. I closed my eyes in the car and leaned my head back, but all I could see were her vacant eyes.

I thought about her family, her father back in Italy who probably didn't know yet. Mainly I thought about how she spent her last night with me, some guy she'd only gotten to know recently. I didn't feel worthy to be the last person with whom she'd spent time.

My head landed heavily on my pillow, but I couldn't get comfortable. I should have been asleep long ago, but my brain was in fifth gear though my body was tired. I was sure the Chapel Hill police chief ran a wonderful department, and that Detective Donnelly was competent at his job. But Buddy Harkin had possessed a relatively low opinion of police departments in general. And apparently that had rubbed off on me. How was I supposed to trust these guys to figure out what was going on?

I thought about the time dad was once falsely accused of conspiracy to commit murder in New York, and therefore kept in a holding cell for thirty-eight hours while a couple of foot soldiers had some fun interrogating him. It was a marathon session until his attorney finally got him out. The net result was a bad bruise on his head and an apology letter from the mayor and chief of police. He had agreed to keep quiet about it, knowing it could always be used to his advantage sometime in the future, when he found himself in need of a favor.

I knew I needed to do something. What would my father do? The only thing I could do was what I'd been trained to do my entire life. Ask the right questions. Find out the truth. Don't give up. Only this time, it wasn't about landing a front page byline in a small town newspaper.

It was about finding the killer of the girl I might have loved.

CHAPTER 7

The next few days were slow and painful. The police were back in touch several more times for statements from each of us. Follow-up questions about what we saw, more details to be reviewed. I'd turned over the tape I had made of our conversation at dinner, which led to even more poking around. How much more can you really remember? But they continued to ask the same things again and again.

There was something I hadn't told them, though. Not because I was trying to hide anything. I hadn't thought about it, at first. Over the past few days, though, since her murder, I kept coming back to it. I actually dreamed about it two nights ago. It would pop into my head when the only thing I was trying to do was get my mind off her for a while. There wasn't anything factual to say about it, which is I guess why I'd withheld it from the detective.

They wanted facts, not feelings. But it was a feeling I had that was getting to me. Something I kept getting stuck on. It was the gut response I had when she spoke about the shroud. There was something mysterious in the way she talked about it. Her demeanor had become nervous and distant. Her eyes darted around the room as she spoke. Her voice lowered. When I got my interview audio tape back from the police, I bet I would be able to hear the change in her voice.

I didn't know why that might be important. It probably wasn't. Just a reporter's hunch. She was bothered by the fact that the shroud was stolen. And I couldn't help but think there was a lot she wasn't telling me.

But a lot she wanted to.

Whatever she had on her mind, I was never going to know. Someone had made sure of that.

I needed to get some air. I grabbed my jacket off of the hook beside the rusty screen door, slid it on, and walked outside, shoving my hands deep into the coat pockets.

That's when I felt it.

A small folded piece of paper with some numbers written neatly. Written in Daniela's handwriting.

Then it hit me. Outside the restaurant. The parking lot. We kissed.

She must have put her hand in my pocket and given me this!

I was staring at a sequence of numbers.

186.55.13.321

I sat down on the steps outside, trying to make sense of them. What was it? A phone number? A bank account?

Maybe she put it there by accident. But that didn't make any sense. No, for some reason she had put this in my pocket on purpose. She wanted me to have it. A code, perhaps?

I barely heard Pasha walk up the gravel driveway toward me.

"Hi, Matthew," he said, startling me out of my trance.

"Hey," I said, waving the scrap of paper in front of his face. "What do you make of these numbers?"

He scanned over them.

"I was thinking maybe some kind of international phone number, maybe bank numbers, or a social security number?"

He held up his hand and shook his head, handing me back the scrap. "No, none of those things," he said.

"You know what they are, then?"

"Sure," he said, walking past me. "It is URL."

He waited for me to understand, and then rolled his eyes impatiently.

"What's that?"

He turned his back to me and walked through the screen door and called back. "A uniform resource locator."

He looked back at me, raising his eyebrows. But that piece of information didn't change the expression of confusion on my face. He sighed.

"That means web address, you American idiot."

CHAPTER 8

I grabbed my laptop and sat down on the sofa in the den. Pasha found a Tab cola, and he sat down beside me.

"What is deal with this URL?"

"You know, your American lingo is improving on a daily basis, Pasha," I said, opening up the computer. "I found this piece of paper in my jacket pocket. I was wearing it the night I was with Daniela for dinner."

Pasha nodded slowly. "You think this is from her?"

I shrugged, but nodded. "When we, you know, kissed in the parking lot, she stuffed her hand in my pocket. I forgot about it until I put on my jacket a second ago. I have this weird feeling she left me this on purpose."

"Why would she do this?" he asked.

I started typing the address. "I hope we find out soon."

Just then, Hoffman came barreling through the front door and saw us sitting together on the sofa, huddled around the laptop.

"Must be something good you boys have there," he said, smirking, and then began rummaging through the refrigerator.

I ignored him, typing in the numbers.

186.55.13.321

A blank screen popped up, with two white spaces in the center.

"There's nothing else on that paper?" asked Pasha.

I glanced at him. "Like a password, you mean?"

"This site is password protected," Pasha said, standing up. "No password, no website."

Hoff was standing over us now, a fresh Diet Coke in hand. We accused him of being a chain smoker at night, and a chain drinker by day. Usually he finished one of the soft drinks just as he was opening up a new one.

I clued him in to the piece of paper I'd found. "Pasha thinks it is some kind of web address."

"I don't think, I know," he said from behind us. "Any guesses as to what her password might be?"

I blinked. He gave me that *well-then-there's-nothing-I-can-do* look, and walked upstairs to his room.

Hoffman patted me hard on the shoulder. "Good luck, bud."

I shrunk down into the couch for a while and tried some passwords. Any combination of words I could think of, from the obvious to the ridiculous.

Portonova

Italy

Shroud

Turin

Talk about looking for a needle in a haystack. I stared at the site, willing it to speak to me.

Lasagna

Nothing. I leaned back, placing my hands behind my head. Whatever was behind this page held the keys to a lot of things. It had to relate to our conversation that night. I recounted it again in my head. It all came back to her work with the Shroud of Turin. The way she talked about it, the excitement in her voice. Everything she knew, up to the recent theft. Her nerves.

She was acting almost like she knew she was being watched.

I slammed the laptop screen shut, threw it in my bag, and jumped off of the sofa.

"Guys, I'll be back later," I yelled, not even waiting for an answer. Swiping my keys from the countertop, I hurried out the door.

CHAPTER 9

I couldn't believe what I was getting ready to do. Something inside was pushing me, though, pressing me forward. I told myself to stop, that I should go to the police, call Detective Donnelly, tell him about the web address. But I couldn't bring myself to do it.

I needed to do something. I had felt so helpless these past few days. Why didn't I do anything to stop him from killing her? I could have yelled at the man. I could have said something. I could have raced up the cliff and maybe stopped Daniela from being murdered right in front of me.

I had to do something. And now I had a chance.

Besides, if I found out anything significant I would take it to the police.

I used all of that logic to justify what I was about to do. In a remote place in the corner of my brain, I wondered if Buddy Harkin had often done the same thing.

I drove to the Wendy's restaurant just off the northeast corner of the campus, grabbed a burger, and mapped out my plan. I also wanted to wait until it got dark. Once it did, I got back into my car, and made my way onto campus.

I parked, grabbed my book bag and hat, and walked. I could easily pass for a graduate student. I came to the Department of Archaeology and Middle Eastern Studies building, Hambright Hall. It was after nine o'clock now and most of the students were back in their dorms, or off to parties, or the library. There was very little happening around this building.

I jiggled the door, hoping to get lucky, but it was locked. So I waited outside the door for someone to come along.

About ten minutes later, a bearded grad student emerged from the building. I quickly walked toward the door, catching it as he came out. *Just act like you're supposed to be here, and no one will know the difference,* I kept telling myself. He was lost in his own archaeological thoughts and barely noticed me enter the building behind him.

I was in. I had my book bag, my alibi, in case anyone should question why I was here so late. Turning in a paper under my professor's door, I would say if asked.

I had been down this hall before, and I knew right where her office was. I turned down the hallway to the left. It was dark, and I stood to listen for a few seconds. No noises. No one seemed to be here. I moved quietly anyway, just in case. Plus, I wasn't exactly used to stealing down hallways at night. My heart rate was jumping.

I stood in front of room 109, telling myself I should have expected this. The name on the plastic placard to the left read "Portonova". Yellow police tape secured the door. They were obviously still investigating her office.

I wasn't sure what the punishment was for tampering with a police crime scene, and I didn't particularly want to find out. But I was here, and it was now or never. I carefully took the tape down and put my hand on the door handle. To my surprise, it turned all the way and the door opened. I had lucked out. Whoever left the office must have figured the tape would scare people away and didn't bother to lock it up.

I had an excuse for being in the building, but not one that would explain why I was in a dead professor's office late at night. So I turned on the lamp in the corner and tried to move fast.

But how do you find someone's password? I began to realize the futility of the search. It may have been locked only in her head, for all I knew. Her old boyfriend's mother's maiden name. Her dog's birthday. Who knew?

I searched around the computer, behind it, and underneath the keyboard. No sticky notes with passwords. I pulled on the file drawers, but they didn't budge. I rolled the middle drawer of her desk slowly open, scanning the contents. Pens, pencils, paperclips, blank stickies. A few Italian coins. Nothing that looked like a password.

Standing in the middle of the office, sweat dripped down my nose. Every second that passed convinced me even more it was not a good idea to be here. I craned my neck to listen for footsteps rushing down the hallway. I pictured a SWAT team securing the perimeter of the building, silently motioning to one another. Soon they'd be slamming me to the tile floor and slapping some handcuffs on my wrists.

I checked behind the pictures on the wall, on the off chance I'd find something there. I assessed the desktop. It was uncluttered, which made me wonder if the police, or an administrative assistant, had cleaned things out already. There was nothing on it.

I sighed, turning around slowly to give the room one more look. I dared not stay any longer. My eyes were drawn to a glass case sitting on her bookshelf. Inside it was a scroll, which appeared to be ancient and very fragile. I ran my finger along the inscription on the case, something written in Hebrew. Carefully I lifted the scroll from the shelf.

A yellow note came unstuck from the bottom, fluttering down through the air. I replaced the scroll and snatched the paper off of the floor. My eyes grew big as I studied it. I snapped a picture on my phone. Replacing the scroll and the note, I silently walked out of the office. I secured the yellow police tape back to the door, scurried down the hallway, and walked outside. I took deep breaths of the fresh air, trying to slow my heart rate.

I made myself walk slowly, but my mind was running. I just may have found what I was looking for.

CHAPTER 10

I found the photo on my phone, set it down beside my laptop, and typed the words into the spaces on the black webpage screen.

Sindone82834

DPortonova

Immediately, a new page appeared, full of information and images.

Across the top were a dozen thumbnail pictures, most of which I couldn't decipher. They appeared to be close-ups of something, taken so close that it was impossible to tell what it was. A few I could recognize, though. They were obviously pictures of the Shroud of Turin.

Below the images, in the middle of the page, were what appeared to be a series of entries that looked like headlines on a blog. They were in fonts of different colors, apparently colored according to the author's name. This was obvious because to the left of the titles were dates, and what looked like usernames in the same color.

There were five names total. I grabbed my small notebook and scribbled them down.

Sindone82834

Becklar79

Textilequeen

Salva316

theophilus

I scrolled down the page and saw that the dates reached back to the first of the year, and the previous year's entries were archived. From what I could gather, the information file contained here appeared to be massive. I saw something and reached for the notebook and my pen again.

Last entry – three days before Daniela died

There was a search function on the left. I played around with it for a minute, typing in random requests. It was apparently set up for the users to research their own site quickly, based on topic, date, or author.

It was the right sidebar of the site, though, that drew my eye. Whoever put together the site had allowed space for some kind of chat room—a way to instant message other users and have a real-time conversation.

I leaned back in my chair, crossing my arms and staring at the screen. My eyes narrowed and I clicked my tongue. Thinking. It was a private research site, designed for a group to share information with only each other. But what was the significance? Did any of this matter?

I reached forward, about to close the laptop, when a message popped up in the chat window.

Becklar79: Daniela?

My eyes widened, and my heart thumped inside my chest. Whoever Becklar79 was, he, or she, thought I was Daniela Portonova.

I tapped on the space bar lightly, not sure what to do. I could pretend to be her, but why? This person may already know she's dead. But maybe not. My hesitation was quickly overtaken by the possibility I could find out something useful.

"Here goes," I mumbled, placing my fingers over the keyboard, and beginning to type.

Who is this?

I tapped my fingers again. No response. I scared him off, I thought to myself. A minute went by. Then another. I sighed, pushing the palms of my hands into my eyes.

When I opened my eyes back up, a message flashed up. Becklar79 had responded.

Where's Daniela? And who are you?

I plucked away at the keys.

A friend.

Should I say anything else? I didn't know who this was and, for all I knew, the bad guys could be on the other end of this conversation. But that didn't make a lot of sense. Odds were this was a colleague. Someone who would want to know what happened. But I needed more from this person.

Who are you?

I waited, and with each passing second with no response, I had the growing feeling I was pushing my luck.

What happened to her?

I shrugged. There was nothing to lose at this point.

Something awful. She was murdered three days ago near her home in Chapel Hill.

I waited a minute, then two, and more.

Are you there, Becklar79? I want to help.

But there was no response. This conversation was over. Becklar79, whoever he was, was gone.

CHAPTER 11

Daniela wanted me to see this site. She gave me the numbers.

I reminded myself of this as I stared at the five usernames again. Sindone82834. Becklar79. Textilequeen. Salva316. Theophilus. Clearly she was the first one. But who was Becklar79? And the others? Colleagues? Fellow shroud researchers?

I tried to click on their names, hoping for some sort of bio to pop up, but no such luck. I knew each of them had uploaded entries into the site. There were various articles, photographs, and notes by each. As I studied the site, it seemed that only one user had no entries whatsoever. The one named Theophilus. I searched, but there was nothing written by him, nothing noted, not even any comments.

The articles were related to the Shroud of Turin in some way. Most were highly technical, and it took all of my concentration to try to decipher them. I noticed, though, there were writings related to archaeological research, explanations debunking various fake-shroud theories, and even some long entries filled with chemical formulas. Chemistry was not my strong suit. I didn't even try to understand those.

Was this some kind of pet project of Daniela's, just a way for her shroud buddies to keep up with each other's research? I was sure there were thousands of sites like it that professors used to share bits and pieces of information with friends around the world.

Maybe this is a simple research site and there's nothing else to it. I tried that idea on for a while to see if it fit. Sometimes, my father would say, the best idea is the most obvious one. Never pursue a truth that doesn't present itself in the evidence, he would say.

But that was it. The evidence itself was nagging at me, whispering in my ear. I tried to step back and be as objective as possible, and when I did, it looked like this:

Daniela Portonova appeared worried and distracted that day. This was my own opinion, of course, but I stood by it. Something was bothering her.

She agreed to do the interview. At the time I thought nothing of it, but there must have been more to the timing than I realized. She wanted to talk, and I was a reporter. Albeit, for a small, local paper, but still. It wasn't the New York Times, but maybe she knew I was investigative by nature.

She was in a hurry, and sometimes people who are desperate take risks.

And the most compelling fact so far—the website itself. She had given me the URL to a private site she used to communicate with a small group of others about the Shroud of Turin. My suspicion was that it was much more than just a shared learning opportunity.

But there were two more facts. First, that the Shroud of Turin was stolen in the middle of the night from its resident church in Italy. It had not turned up, no one had claimed responsibility, no one had been caught, and no ransom had been demanded. The authorities were dumbfounded. The shroud had simply vanished. It was clearly a professional job.

And second, not long after, one of the foremost shroud scholars in the world was murdered in cold blood, shot twice and pushed off a cliff.

The authorities had proposed all kinds of theories regarding Daniela's murder. They ranged from straightforward robbery and homicide, to an utterly ridiculous theory put forward by one investigator that involved the mafia and her family connections somehow catching up with her.

Robbery made no sense, though. Why would she be robbed, then driven to a cliff and shot? The mafia theory, of course, was laughable. Someone had been watching too many episodes of the Sopranos. They seemed to be landing on the idea that it was some sort of sexual assault crime. The autopsy, however, had produced no signs whatsoever of this.

I opened up a full-screen picture of the shroud from the site. The image was grainy, but looking closely, I could see the body of a man with a beard. He appeared to have been beaten, perhaps crucified, and laid to rest. The man on the fabric and I stared at each other and questions began to form in my mind.

Are the theft of the shroud and Daniela's murder really somehow intertwined?

Who are these four other people on the website? Do any of them have anything to do with her death?

Did one of them do it?

What was the purpose of this group of five professors, or scientists, or archeologists, or whoever they were? Beyond their common interest in the shroud, was there another reason they were together?

I knew when I got this way it was useless to try to stop my brain from tumbling these questions and facts over and over. It's just how I'm wired, I guess. On top of that, I'm one stubborn individual. Another trait I have my father to thank for, of course.

All of which meant I couldn't put any of this aside. I had questions. I needed answers.

Daniela deserved that.

CHAPTER 12

When I was eight years old my dad came home from overseas to see us for a few months. To understand the great Buddy Harkin, you needed to know that he never, ever did anything halfway. It wasn't in his nature. He was loud, hilariously funny, a whirlwind of scotch-fueled energy. It irritated mom to see him swoosh home, create chaos, lavish us with exotic presents, and then whisk himself right through the door again, as quickly as he had come.

He charmed her, too, though. That was their magic, their chemistry. She would act put out with him, but he would grab her and whirl her around the room, with her screaming "Stop it, stop it!" and my sister and I chasing them around, whooping and hollering.

As a kid, the day he came home always felt like Christmas, even if it were in the heat of the summer.

"I'm going to take you fishing tomorrow." Those were his first words to me that day as he leaned down to speak to me at eye-level. "You think you can handle some fishing with your old man?"

"Buddy," mom said, "are you sure he's old enough to do that sort of thing?"

I was thinking, *Old enough to go fishing? Come on, mom!* But she knew a fishing trip with my dad was not like other fathers who walk their sons down to the lake with a pole and a can of worms, trying to catch a few bream or maybe a bass if they were lucky.

"Nonsense," dad said. "Mattie is plenty old enough to go with me and the boys."

She frowned. *The boys.* A ragtag assortment of dad's friends that mom didn't approve of. She muttered something under her breath, but said nothing, which was approval enough for me.

Little did I know fishing with dad meant an early-morning plane ride. We hopped on a small jet down to

North Carolina, rented a car and made a bee line for the Outer Banks, a rim of remote barrier islands along the coast. Dad's friends were loud, funny, and used words my mother had forbidden my sister and I to say. I loved it. I beamed at my dad, driving us down the road.

He had arranged for us to do some blue marlin fishing off the coast. He hired the best captain and crew in the area and, before I knew it, the thirty-two foot Happy Blue was pointing eastward, out into the Atlantic.

"Hey Buddy, is your boy Matt going to be able to handle these big fish?" I could hear one of dad's friends ask him.

Dad walked over and put his hand on my head and shook it. "One hundred dollars says that Mattie here catches the biggest marlin on the boat." I wore a grin a mile wide for the rest of the day.

The captain found the right spot, and my rod suddenly began to bend and shake violently. I had actually hooked one.

"Okay, boy," the mate said, "you're up first!" He sat me down in the chair and handed me the rod. It almost flew out of my hands, but I held on tight.

Whatever it was on the other end of that line, I was in for a fight. I battled that fish for the next hour. My eight-year-old hands were small. But every time someone offered to help, I didn't say anything, just shook my head no.

Pretty soon my fingers started bleeding. The tension on the line and the cold wind were cutting through my flesh. But I was reeling the fish in. Slowly, I was bringing him closer and closer to us. I was winning.

Every time I started to waver, I looked back up at my dad, who was standing behind me, chatting. He would see the tired look in my eyes and say, "Come on, Mattie! You're a Harkin! Harkins are strong, we persevere, we never give up! You can do it, Mattie!"

My hands were really burning now, though. Tears formed in my eyes. But I was going to make sure my dad won that bet.

Just as I was about to pass out, the first mate gaffed the fish and hauled him into the boat. I had never seen such a beast. He had a sword for a nose and his scales glistened as he flopped on the deck. He was the biggest fish I'd ever seen.

My dad pulled out his wallet and handed me a crisp, new hundred.

"Atta boy, Mattie. You stuck with it. No one's going to catch anything bigger'n that," he said, tousling my hair again. I don't remember much more about the fish. But I remembered that my father was proud of me. And I can't recall a better feeling in all of my childhood years.

Sometimes you have to stick through things, through the pain, beyond the bloody fingers. Because you know that what you really want you can't have unless you go through some hurt.

I had that feeling today, that I was starting to reel something in. And that it was going to be a long journey. One that could even get painful. I remembered what it felt like to persevere.

This was bigger than anything I'd been a part of before. I was in a boat, floating on the vast expanse of ocean, realizing for the first time I had no anchor. I'd never needed one before. I'd been my own. But I felt the mooring come loose inside. I was adrift. To where, I did not know.

CHAPTER 13

A man stared at himself in the mirror above the sink in the motel room just off of Franklin Street, a few miles away from the university campus. His hair was closely cropped and platinum blond, thanks to the Revlon dyeing kit now stuffed in the trash. His long hair was in the garbage, too. He admired his new look, rubbing his gaunt, chiseled face.

Three small round wounds stood out on the right side of his stomach, and a four-inch scar across his shoulder. He had to look closely to see them. A myriad assortment of tattoos covered the faint images.

He pushed his fingers through his hair. He didn't like it, but it would have to do for a while. Until he got out of this place and back home. Besides, he'd done it a dozen times before or after a job like this. Changed his look, often his hairstyle, sometimes going as far as adding a false beard or moustache. It always amazed him how much one small change could affect his appearance and could throw off anyone who might have seen him before.

He slid on the black, horn-rimmed glasses and his transformation was complete. It would almost be time to finish the job and get out of here. It couldn't come too soon as far as he was concerned. A few more items of business to attend to, then he was ready to go home and disappear. And get paid.

He opened his passport, studying his new identity. Brandin Mueller. He wondered how many different names he'd had. It was impossible to count. Some days he'd almost forgotten his given name, and had to repeat it to himself.

Andrea Benito.

Benito walked across the room with a detached sense of economy. No movement wasted, every move calculated. Silently he dressed and headed out the door.

Chapel Hill was a good place to remain anonymous. There were freaks and geeks of every variety walking around downtown, and it put the man at ease. Why would anyone notice him when every third person he passed had green or purple hair and no less than three face and body piercings? On cue, a six-foot six guy with a rainbow-spiked Mohawk came around the corner, walking beside a girl with a shaved head and swirled tattoo across the left side of her face.

"Crazy American students," he muttered, walking on.

He found a student newspaper and stepped inside the Starbucks for an espresso of which he took one sip and almost cursed out loud. He shook his head. No one knew how to make a good espresso here. If circumstances were different, perhaps he would move to America and open his own coffee shop and show Starbucks how to do it.

But indeed, it seemed that would have to wait for a while. Maybe another lifetime. His current career path was all-consuming. It had taken him across the world. And he had met some interesting people. Some good, others very, very bad. Some he liked, others he couldn't stand. It was no matter to him. They ended up dead eventually.

Benito sat down in a comfortable leather chair, crossed his legs, and opened up the newspaper. Around him were college students drinking four-dollar lattes they put on their parent-sponsored expense accounts, gabbing away at each other. The paper was from the week before and contained the usual liberal college town rants about politics, the environment, and the evils of the capitalist system. Bypassing these, he came to an article called "Campus Projects Progressing" and stopped. It was written by Matthew Harkin, his picture below the headline.

Nice looking guy, he thought, as he took another sip of his watered-down espresso. *Too bad.*

He folded up the paper, placed it inside his jacket pocket, and looked at his watch. Time to go.

Standing up, he walked back on the street, narrowly avoiding being hit by a speeding bicyclist, and briskly made his way back to the motel. It was time to make the last preparations and get ready for a busy evening.

CHAPTER 14

"What's going on up here, dude?" Hoffman's head popped up through the trap door in the roof of my old house. There were three small stools sitting on the flat landing directly above the back porch. One of the quirky things about my place was the rooftop gathering spot, just big enough for the three of us.

I was smoking a Cuban cigar courtesy of Hoff's father, sitting with my back against the wall. This was where I came to get my head straight, to clear the fog and to think. I found that a fine cigar always helped. I didn't smoke cigarettes, I didn't drink a lot of alcohol. But in the past few years I had come to love the taste of a cigar. I blew a smoke ring into the air and watched it drift aimlessly upward, admiring my skill.

"Those things will kill you, you know," said Hoff, as he whipped one out of his shirt pocket and lit it.

"Your dad is a fine, fine man," I said, admiring the cigar in my fingers.

"Oh yeah, he's a real treat. Be glad he's not your dad."

There was an awkward silence. I could tell he immediately regretted those words.

The blue smoke curled up against the cool starlit sky and we both sat for a few minutes, our eyes gazing upward. It was almost enough to make me forget for a few minutes all that had happened in the last week.

I felt Hoffman's eyes studying me.

"What?"

He blew a ring of his own and pushed his hair back out of his eyes. "You have that look, man."

"What are you talking about?"

"I don't know. Just a wild look in your eyes. What are you planning?"

I tried to pretend I didn't know what he was talking about. Even though I'd been thinking about what I could do next to help find Daniela's killer. "Got no plans. Where are you getting this from?"

"You just look like you do sometimes when we play basketball. Remember that time in college? We were down at Woollen gym and were playing those grad student losers who were beating us pretty good, and Pasha came up with a bloody nose because one of the guys smashed his elbow in his face? And you had this look on your face, man, like 'you dudes can get the hell out of my way.'"

"Yeah," I said, sighing. "I seem to recall something like that." A sometimes illogical stubbornness is not a quality I love about myself. I blamed it on my dad.

Hoff continued, starting to laugh. "The next time down you took the ball. You demanded it, really. You dribbled around until you found the guy who gave it to Pasha, you drove right into him and, as you're going up, you slam the ball into the guy's face. Just so he can have a bloody nose, too."

"I remember," I said, quietly. "It didn't end well."

"Uh, no." A full-fledged fistfight ensued, and campus police kicked us out of the gym for a week.

Hoff puffed on the stogie again. "That look you have in your eyes. That's where I've seen it before. So, I ask you again, what are you planning?"

I turned to him, my voice was unnaturally calm.

"I'm going to find the people who did this to Daniela. I'm going to figure out what's going on, and what part these people on this website have to play in it. I'm going to track them all down. There are other people who are going to get hurt if someone doesn't figure out what's going on." And for final measure, whether it was my bravado, or the cigar speaking, I said, "And I am going to make whoever was responsible for this pay."

He looked at me out of the corner of his eyes. I expected a sarcastic comment, but I got nothing but silence.

"Okay, Mattie boy," Hoff finally said. "I'm here to help."

We heard a clunking sound coming up the wooden ladder and saw a hand shoot out of the trap door, carrying a laptop, which was placed gingerly on the cigar ash-covered floor. Pasha emerged, coughed a few times and swatted away the smoke.

"That is filthy habit," he scolded, but his eyes twinkled. A smile curled on his lips, which was quite uncommon for Pasha Griecko.

"What are you so giddy about?"

He sat down on a stool and opened up his laptop on his knees. The blue screen glowed on his face in the dark, making him look all mad scientist-like. Clearly he had found something of interest.

"I have been looking through your website for past two hours," he said. "There is much, much information here. All on this Shroud of Turin, everything you could ever want to know about it. History, theories, its origin, the—"

I interrupted. "Yes, Pasha, I know, I know. Lots of articles and diagrams and research. I saw it."

"Let me finish, Matthew," he said, pushing his glasses back up to the bridge of his nose. "I could only scan a little of it, but there are some very interesting ideas here. Enough that I think there is more to this than, as you say, meets the eye. But also, I do some digging behind the website itself."

Hoff raised his hand, sitting on the deck with his legs crossed. In the darkness he looked more like a kid in class with a question. Minus the glowing cigar. "What does that mean?"

Pasha sighed. "I look at architecture behind site. How code was written, trying to understand who is webmaster, who maintains the site. I figure, whoever keeps up a site like this must be close to these people."

"Or maybe even one of them?" I offered.

Pasha nodded. "Perhaps. I look at where site is registered and who it is registered to. Highly unusual, but this information I cannot access. This is public data, but for some reason there is technical error when I try to trace this."

"Maybe just a computer error," I said.

"Or your hacking skills need some help," said Hoff, inhaling on the cigar.

If you want to insult Pasha, start talking about his computer skills. He brushed his hand in front of him, like he was swatting a fly. "I hack into top secret chess program in mainframe of University of Moscow when I was thirteen. Trust Pasha, it is not my lack of skills." He glared at Hoffman, folding his arms over his chest.

"Okay, okay," I said, trying to get him back on track. "So?"

"So," he relented, "I try to get around this but information has been erased. Highly unusual, as I said. Someone is trying hard to cover tracks. They seem paranoid. But I looked at the code more closely. Embedded in it are certain markers."

"What do you mean, markers?" I asked.

"Certain types of code are germane to certain parts of the world. Much like a dialect in a language. Programmers in Asia have different style than in North America, who have different approach than Europe, and so on. This to me is clearly European-oriented website."

"Well," Hoffman said, "great. We've narrowed it down to an entire continent. What next, Columbo?"

"Let me finish, you moron." Moron was his new American word for the week. I thought he had been using it quite effectively. "So I access European database, and search for similar coding structures that would parallel the website—"

Both Hoffman and I sighed loudly at the same time.

"Get to the point, Pasha. Please. What did you find?" I asked.

"Look at this and tell me what you see." He furiously typed in a web address to the browser. Up popped a site. The three of us hovered over the computer in the darkness. It was a site for the religion department.

At the University of Cambridge.

"Read over home page," Pasha said, sitting back against the wall, closing his eyes, "and tell what you find."

I scanned it quickly. Information about the programs, the school, ongoing research. And at the very bottom in a small, grey font, one sentence: *"This site maintained by Larry Beckham, associate professor of religion, and webmaster."*

Larry Beckham. It clicked.

"Larry Beckham…Becklar79…that has to be the guy I chatted with. That's him!" I slapped Pasha on the leg. "Pasha, you're brilliant."

"Dah," he nodded, smiling. "I am brilliant."

CHAPTER 15

"So what do you do, just call the guy up?"

Hoffman flicked his ashes over the railing.

"How's that going to go?" I asked. "Hi, you don't know me and I don't know you, but this woman you've been working with, well, she got killed, and I saw it. Do you know anything about it? Did you help do it?"

I thought for a minute. "See, that's just the thing. For all we know, any one of those people on the website may be involved in her death."

"How do you know that?" asked Hoff. "Are you some kind of conspiracy theorist or something? Maybe the police have it right after all. It's their job, you know. Maybe it was just a robbery that went terribly wrong. Or God forbid, but maybe it was an actual sexual assault situation. She puts up a big fight, and he decides to just get rid of her. So he takes her to the cliff…"

"But that doesn't explain how she was acting that day," I said, breaking in. "The police think it's just a local crime. It clearly seems bigger than that to me. And you weren't with her. I was. There was something going on. She was worried. She talked to me about the Shroud of Turin being stolen. She was concerned about it. And another thing. She acted strange in the restaurant. Like she was looking for somebody. Or really, she acted like somebody was looking for her. She kept glancing around."

"With all due respect," said Hoff, "there could have been a million things she was worried about. Maybe she had a tough conversation with her supervisor. Or trouble with her family back home. Or she just wasn't feeling well. Look, I'm on your side here, like I said. I'm just trying to get you to see this from another angle."

I conceded his point. "That's possible. But a couple of things stand out to me. She seemed to know something about the shroud being stolen. More than she was saying. I've played the conversation over and over again in my mind. She was bothered by something. And then there is the issue of the website itself. Why in the world would she stuff that in my pocket and take off?"

The three of us pondered these things out on the deck. I was quickly drawn to the only logical conclusion I could come up with.

"I need to treat this like an investigation. Like a story." I said this out loud, but almost to myself. "What would I do if I were investigating this like a lead? I would track down each of these people, one by one, and try to interview them. Now let's assume that one of two things is true. First, that this Larry Beckham guy is quite possibly involved in her murder. He is, for obvious reasons, going to avoid phone conversations with Americans from Chapel Hill at all costs. We want to actually find him and talk to him. Not scare him off."

"And second option?" Pasha asked.

"The second option is that Beckham is in the same boat Daniela was," I suggested. "Worried, scared this could happen to him, too. Either way, we're not getting Mr. Beckham on the phone for a friendly chat."

"What are you saying, Matthew? Are you going to go to Cambridge, find his house, and knock on his door? 'Hi, how are you? Can I come in for a few minutes?'"

I looked at Pasha, then over to Hoff, and cleared my throat. "Maybe. But I was kind of hoping I could have some company."

"You are crazy," Pasha said, folding his arms again. "You want us to go to England with you? I cannot go anywhere. I have computer science exam tomorrow, lab on next day…"

Hoffman, who had been unusually quiet for a few minutes, took out his wallet. He opened the fold of dark leather and thumbed behind five or six credit cards until he found one stuffed at the back. He pulled out a black card, and held it up in front of us.

"Do you guys know what this is?" he asked, a grin on his face.

Pasha blinked. "It is black credit card. So what?"

"Not just any credit card, Pasha, my Kazakh friend. This is a black American Express. It's my father's card. It has no limit." He stopped to let that sink in. "No credit limit, gentlemen. Do you know that last year Kanye bought his Gulfstream V using a black American Express? Do you know that Master P filled up his garage with Bentleys using a card like this?"

"Your father still gives you a credit card?" Pasha asked.

We both ignored the question, but I eyed him warily. "What are you saying, Hoff? You want to be a rap star?"

"Just travel like one," he said, his eyes twinkling. "Who wants to book a flight to London tonight?"

"Your dad would be furious," I said. Even though the idea sounded great to me, I didn't want him to feel the wrath of a rich, angry father.

He picked his cigar back up and sat down. His face grew serious again. "Dad's already furious. Screw him. I'm not going to let you do something like this on your own. You've stood by me before, you know."

I raised my eyebrows and measured the earnestness on his face. He met my gaze and nodded.

Pasha was already reluctantly pecking away at his keyboard.

"How soon do you want to leave?" he asked.

"You mean 'we,' don't you, Pasha?" Hoff sat up and slapped him on the shoulder. "I think you owe Mattie here too. If it weren't for him you wouldn't have any friends. You'd have moved back home by now, isn't that what you told me?"

Pasha said nothing but breathed out heavily.

I glanced at him. I'd never heard that before. It made me shift uncomfortably on the deck.

Hoff caught my eye and winked, knowing Pasha's sigh was a resigned yes.

"There is 12:43AM flight tonight, but surely not so soon." He looked at his watch. "That's two hours."

"Let's do it," Hoffman announced. He was more fired up now than I was. Maybe his recent argument with his dad was fueling his desire to blow up his credit card.

"There are only first class tickets available, from Raleigh-Durham airport…they are two thousand dollars each."

Hoff didn't blink. "Book it."

Pasha looked unbelievingly at me.

I was grinning. "You heard the man, Pasha. Let's book the flight. Three tickets."

"Dah, okay," Pasha said, taking the card from Hoffman and plugging in the information. We watched as he clicked away. "Three tickets…booked."

I stood up. "Alright, boys. Get your passports. Let's get packed. We're heading to England."

CHAPTER 16

Benito parked the police cruiser in front of Matthew Harkin's listed address. Silently he moved behind the car, opened the trunk and reached into a black leather duffel. He removed a forty-five caliber Glock and screwed the silencer onto the end, placing it in his holster.

Shutting the trunk, he surveyed the scene around him, waiting. No movement up and down the street. It was empty. He shoved his hands in his pockets and walked toward the small house. Not many homes were within earshot, which was good. *This is going to be easy,* he thought. *This police uniform should help. Get in, do the job, get out. Go home.*

He had lost track of how many jobs just like this he had done. He knew what to expect, and he knew preparation was the key. His client wanted very little mess left, and no evidence. The clients he had worked with were as unique as the jobs he had done. This time, however, his relationship with his employer was…different. He had been approached from an unexpected source. An old acquaintance. With an unusual request.

He thought about his home, thousands of miles away. The expansive winery he now owned looked over the village, the streets he used to roam as an aimless, impoverished youth in the southern end of Rome. He had grown up carousing through its back alleys. Over time, those narrow streets chiseled his violent skill into something useful. Each day at his home reminded him of where he had been and how far he had come. He had parlayed his violent education into a lucrative career.

It was on his white stone terrace overlooking the city that he had been visited by his old friend.

Father Paniti stole quietly through the double doors of the house and onto the patio. Quickly the man rose and greeted his dear old friend and priest. The Father was dressed plainly in his brown cleric's robe with no adornments. The man bent down and kissed the priest's hand, ushering him in to sit down and have some tea.

He was intrigued by this visit. It had been at least five years since he had seen the Father. But speaking with him this morning reminded him of his childhood, how he considered the priesthood himself at one point, and how Father Paniti had saved him from the black hole of the streets, from himself. His family was faithful to the church and to Paniti. He was family.

"Benito," the Father said, leaning back in his chair, sipping his tea, "your help is needed."

He listened intently as the old priest explained his needs. It was very simple, really. A list of people, complete with pictures. Some travel involved. Quick. Professional. No traces, no mess. His specialty. Benito was certainly happy to lend his services. And his interest was more than piqued when it became abundantly clear money was of no object.

Benito thought about this as he stood in front of his target's house. He didn't want to let his good friend down, not now. He felt the adrenaline begin to course through his veins. He slowed his breathing accordingly, willing himself to calm down.

He lowered the brim of his hat and stepped up onto the front porch, his hand fingering the gun at his side. There were small windows on either side of the door. He casually peeked inside, but saw no movement. A lamp was on, but there were no signs of life in the house.

This was a problem. He saw only one car parked in the carport and wasn't sure what that meant. How many were inside? Ideally, it was only Matthew Harkin, though he had taken the presence of the roommates into account. He didn't work in a world of ideals, though, but of cold, hard realities. He'd had enough experience to know the ideal situation rarely presented itself. If there were others inside, so be it. There was almost always collateral damage.

The question was, how to get in. Or maybe, how to get them to come out and play. Always choosing the direct approach, Benito raised his hand to the door.

Tap. Tap. Tap. Benito calmly knocked.

No one came.

He tried again, this time, a little louder. Again, no response.

One more time, he knocked, even louder.

"Open up," he said in a low voice. "This is the police."

Maybe I'm still not being direct enough, Benito thought. He pulled out a long, thin piece of metal from his coat pocket and had the door open in less than three seconds.

Come out, come out, wherever you are. He walked in with his gun raised.

CHAPTER 17

Pasha had been the first to spot the tall, thin man with the horn-rimmed glasses in the police uniform, eyeing our residence carefully, and then stopping at the end of the driveway, under one of the oaks. We were still on the roof, overlooking the back of the house. I crawled up the pitched section, the rough asphalt shingles burning my knees, but I tried to stay as flat as I could. Reaching the peak, I peered over, hiding behind the chimney, I had a clearer view of the officer.

I soaked in as many details as I could. Platinum blond, closely-cropped hair sticking out under his hat. A chiseled, serious face. He was wearing a police uniform.

On any normal night, I would go downstairs and just greet the guy at the door. Sirens were going off in my head, though.

It was the image of his silhouette as he stepped against the street light that made me freeze.

"What do you see?" Hoff asked, with a loud whisper. I held up my finger, and scooted myself back down the roof and onto the deck.

Neither one of us had seen the face of the man who killed Daniela. His features had been blurred by distance, frustrating the detectives, who had grilled us over and over again. An arm with a gun, a flash of a silhouette against the night sky, the sound of a weapon discharging.

"I think it's him," I told them as I jumped down from the room. "He's wearing a police uniform, but I think it's him."

"Him?" Hoff cocked his head. "By 'him', you mean…"

I nodded. "The killer."

"No one saw him, Matt," Hoffman whispered, glancing back over his shoulder. "Why do you think that?"

"His silhouette, the hair, his face," I said. I paused. "And a gut feeling. Everybody needs to stay right here, against the wall, and whatever you do, don't move. He'll never see us up here, and if he's just an officer, he'll go away and come back in the morning."

Pasha's eyes had grown wider than I'd ever seen them. "And if he is killer?"

I raised my eyebrows and didn't say anything. We stood on the overlook, our backs against the brick wall of the house.

We listened.

Silence.

Then, the slow crunching of feet against gravel. The footsteps continued, only louder, and then we heard him step onto the front porch. I slowly turned my head to look at Hoffman and Pasha. Hoff was looking down, his breathing growing quick and shallow. Pasha was literally shaking. I reached out and grabbed his hand, and he shaking lessened.

I felt my own hands begin to twitch. The idea that Daniela's killer might be outside our home caused my mind to race.

I snuck back to the top of the roof, peering over the edge. I saw his blue police cap in front of the door. He knocked, several times. A few seconds later, I heard a metallic sliding sound, and the creak of the door opening.

Just like that, he was inside our house. I slid back down to the deck.

"Hoff," I whispered. "Do you have your car keys?"

He reached into his pocket and pulled them out, holding them up for me to see.

"Okay," I said. "We have to go, *now*. Follow me."

I climbed back onto the roof and motioned for them to come. They scrambled up after me, and we moved our feet as softly as possible until we got to the peak. We tiptoed across the top until we were standing on the edge, looking down at the carport.

It was five feet over, and probably six feet down onto the carport roof. From where we were standing, though, it looked like a cliff jump.

"We need to do this, guys," I whispered, and, before they could protest, I jumped, landing with both feet on the flat surface. I looked back up at Pasha's scared face, wondering for a second if he was going to be able to do it. But he willed himself off of the edge, falling down beside me. Behind him came Hoffman, slamming into the smaller rooftop, sprawling out in front of us, moaning in pain.

We sat frozen, terrified the man would burst out of the side door of the house before we could get to the car. I was sure he must have heard the thudding against the carport roof. The three of us shimmied down the basketball hoop beside the carport roof and hit the gravel. Scrambling, we climbed into Hoff's Jeep as he fumbled with the keys.

"Hoffman, come on, let us get out of here now!" Pasha's voice was a high-pitched squeal I hadn't heard before. Any other time, it would have been very amusing.

The car roared and Hoffman jammed it in reverse, pressing hard on the accelerator. Gravel spewed from under the tires, but at this point we didn't care.

We were almost to the top of the driveway when I saw the screen door at the side of the house fly open. It was him, with the same calm, steely look on his face, his arm pointed toward us.

In his hand was a pistol.

"He's gonna shoot!" Hoff shrieked.

The man fired. Two bullets pierced the windshield. We ducked, and Hoffman backed the car out wildly, somehow finding the street while barely able to look out the window. As he slammed it into drive, three more bullets hit the passenger window and the side of the car. Glass rained over us, hard, and we were all screaming. Hoff stood on the accelerator. The car lurched forward.

I looked up just enough to see the man running up the driveway, hat flying off of his head, holding his gun as if about to shoot again, staring at the car. Instead of shooting, though, he pocketed his weapon and then ran in the opposite direction.

"Is everybody okay?" I shouted.

"Dah, dah," said Pasha, brushing his dirty pants off. "I'm fine."

"I'm okay," Hoff said, craning his neck to look in the rearview mirror. "But he shot my car! With real bullets! Are you kidding me? Jesus!"

I glanced back. "I don't want to be a downer here, but I saw him running back the other way. I think he was going for his car."

There was no sign of a car following us. Yet. Hoffman hit the gas so the Jeep literally jumped down Franklin Street, heading toward the interstate.

"Turn down here," I said, motioning to a cut-through road. Chances were this guy was not as familiar with the roads as we were. Maybe we would have an advantage on the back roads. "This will take us through a neighborhood and over a couple of streets. Then we can get on the next interchange down and hit the interstate."

Hoffman took the road. "What if he finds us? He's going to track us down, guys." Panic rose into his throat. "He's going to kill us, just like the professor. Maybe we should just go to the police station."

"The real police?" I said. "Would you really trust them now? What if someone in the department is in on it? If we really want to get away from him, I say we stick to our plans."

Pasha looked at me like I had grown a third eye. "You mean continue on to the airport? Are you crazy?"

"Look," I said, my voice raised, "it's been over a week since we witnessed a murder in front of our very eyes and they aren't any closer to catching the killer than they were the night she dropped out of the sky right in front of us.

Not only did they not catch him, now this guy dressed up as a police officer is trying to kill *us*."

"But we know what the killer looks like now," Pasha said. "We can identify him. They can print flyers and pass around the town."

"Look, Pasha, I just don't think the police are—"

"Hey guys," Hoffman said, his voice tensing up as he watched the rearview mirror again. "You may not want to see this, but I think he's found us!"

Our heads swiveled around and we saw a police car gaining on us quickly down the neighborhood street. His lights were on and the siren was blaring. The killer's determined face was planted behind the steering wheel.

"Hoff," I said. "Come on, man. Get us out of here!"

"Hold on." Hoffman stepped on the gas. His Jeep responded quickly and we were pushed back into our seats. A stack of compact discs came out of a low-hanging compartment and rolled around on the floor.

"He is coming fast," said Pasha.

"Just another mile and we're going to be at the interstate," Hoff said.

"Based on how fast it looks like he is moving, we may not have another mile," I said.

The man was now close enough that I could see him clearly. With his left hand he held the steering wheel. With his right he held up a gun, pointing it to the ceiling of his car. He wasn't able to shoot it, but he wanted us to know he still had it and would use it when he was in range. Not that we needed reminding.

Hoffman was doing an admirable job of driving under pressure, considering the circumstances. Which meant he was keeping it on the road and out of people's yards.

"Take a left up here!" I shouted, realizing a the short-cut was coming up quickly.

Hoff slowed and then jerked the car down the side street. The jeep lunged to the right but maintained its balance. I looked back in time to see the cruiser slam on the brakes and skid, almost missing the turn, narrowly avoiding a telephone pole. But he was soon back behind us, closing in.

We turned again, this time onto a city street that had a few cars on it. I noticed he slowed his pursuit, keeping a safe distance between him and us. Just ahead, the interstate ramp bore to the right. Hoff squealed onto the ramp and in seconds we were on the four-lane blacktop heading east.

The man was content to leave a certain distance between us and him on the freeway. There were more cars out now. Hoffman settled into the middle lane. The man seemed as if he wanted to wait it out, follow us until we decided to get off the interstate and back onto a more deserted, secondary road.

I looked back again and he actually waved his gun at me. I could see a slight grin on his face.

"Hoffman," I said, "head to the airport."

"What?"

"The airport. Let's go."

"Great idea, Matt. Let's just head to the airport. Maybe he can follow us in. Maybe we can even get an extra ticket for the terminator and we can all go on holiday in London together!"

"No, no, listen," I said. "We drive to the airport. He follows us, but he will have no choice but to stop. Where else is safer than an airport these days? Cops everywhere. What do you think he's going to do, shoot us there?"

"And then what, Mr. Genius?" said Pasha. "We just get on airplane and fly away?"

"Yeah, why not?" I said. "Got any better ideas?"

Both of them were quiet. I figured it was because they both knew it could actually work. At least on the airplane, we could buy ourselves some time to get away, I mean really get away, and figure some things out. We had Daniela's killer after us. That reality had sunk in. I just needed some time to sort it out. I needed a chance to find the right people to help us.

"Well," Hoff said, "we better get there in a hurry, then." He sped up and began to pass people on the left and right, never staying in the same lane for long. The police car sped up with us, but remained several car lengths back. I saw his face, though, and it was clear he did not know what to make of this.

It was not until we reached the airport exit that he appeared to have figured out where we were going. That meant that the best time, the only time, to kill us was now. He began gaining ground. Hoffman drove valiantly, but the Jeep was no match for the souped up cruiser. He tore in and out of lanes, cutting in front of drivers, causing the man to swerve back and forth to keep up. His gun was up and his window was down, ready for a clean shot. I imagined a bullet ripping into our tire. We would be sent hurtling across the highway, off a bridge or into oncoming traffic.

But Hoffman kept him off balance. The man simply could not manage to get a shot off. And soon we were slowing down at the airport entrance. We were now side by side with a half dozen cars, being funneled to the front of the airport. The sedan edged slowly up beside us. He had pocketed his gun.

He stared at us. A cold, dark face. As if to say he would be waiting for us when we left the airport.

Of course, how could he have known we had tickets to fly to England that very night?

CHAPTER 18

We sat down in the plush first-class seats on a remarkably uncrowded British Airways 757 Airbus. I had never sat in first class before, but I was in a daze from our journey to the airport and almost unaware of the flurry of flight attendants around us. Drinks, food, pillows, blankets, more pillows.

How about a suitcase full of clothes? I almost said. I leaned my head back on the seat, closed my eyes, and began to rub my temples. None of us had time to pack anything. Between the three of us, we had Pasha's laptop and the clothes on our backs. The thought of Hoff's black American Express card eased my mind a bit. He had already informed us the first thing we would do when we hit London was to go shopping. If I knew Hoff, we were heading for some very expensive store.

"Fine," Pasha said. "but I don't want to look like Abercrombie and Fitch model."

"Or a fedora-wearing pimp from the big city," I added.

We sat in silence. I needed the time to digest everything. The adrenaline rush had been pushing us for the past hour, and now the physical crash we experienced was just as dramatic. The only high-speed chases I'd ever been in happened back as a college student on my mountain bike, trying to make it to class on time. And, generally speaking, even though I would take curves and jump down steps at breakneck pace, my life was never in danger.

He fired a gun at us. He was trying to kill us.

That thought nestled uncomfortably into a dark corner of my brain. I eyed Pasha and Hoffman and knew they were thinking the same. I found myself gripping the hand rests tightly as I processed the escape from our house, and then the car chase to the airport. I forced myself to relax, breathing deeply, easing up on my death grip.

Hoffman was sitting on the aisle seat, his mouth gaping open, already beginning to snore.

Pasha was staring out the window into the dark night sky. I thought about what it must feel like to be thousands of miles from home. What it would have felt like to be chased and almost killed if I was in Moscow instead of Chapel Hill.

I would want to see my mother. I would want to feel safe again.

The plane now flattened its climb out as we hit our cruising altitude. I closed my eyes and fell, half-dreaming, into an old memory. I was twelve-years-old, and it was the day that a brown paper package arrived at our doorstep. It was addressed to me and had a return address from somewhere in Israel. At that age, I got excited about junk mail sent to Current Resident. So a mysterious package from the Middle East was something huge. My mother handed the package to me with a concerned smile. She knew something she wasn't telling me.

I tore it open, and three items fell to the floor. An envelope with fifteen crisp hundred dollar bills, a world map, and a note from my dad. The note said simply: "Mattie, meet me at the Grand Hyatt Hotel in Cairo in three days. I'll be waiting for you. Love, Dad." I looked inside the envelope and thumbed slowly through the money. Then I opened up the map. He had highlighted the city of Cairo with a yellow marker. That was it.

A day and a half later I was on a flight I had booked myself, all the way to Egypt. He gave me no other details. Since this was before the internet age, I made phone calls to travel agencies and planned my own itinerary. I memorized it, knowing my schedule down to the minute. I packed one bag, meticulously, trying to prepare for any adventure possible. It was scary, and further away from home than I had ever been before, especially alone. I loved every minute of it.

Now, as I nodded off, my mind raced through that trip. From the airplane ride, where I was doted on by all of the stewardesses, who couldn't believe I was being allowed to make a trip like this on my own, to the disorienting feeling of being around thousands of Egyptians and others from far corners of the world at the massive Cairo airport. To the crazy taxi driver who almost mowed over a camel. Crisply etched in my memory was getting out of the cab, paying the driver, and walking up the steps to the Grand Hyatt Cairo. I was halfway around the world and I had made it on my own.

I remember walking in through the expansive, marble-floored lobby, in which everything seemed to have been polished, shined, and scrubbed. I must have been walking around with my mouth hanging open, because I saw a man sitting on a soft, leather sofa drop his newspaper and say, "Boy, you are going to catch flies with your mouth that wide open!" I turned to see dad sitting there, reading glasses on, cigar in mouth.

"Welcome to Cairo," he said, as if I might have just as easily been meeting him at the bagel shop down the street from our New York apartment. I ran over and wrapped my arms around his neck. I had enjoyed the adventure of the plane trip on my own, but I had to admit I was glad to see my father at the end of this journey. We spent a week there together, exploring the pyramids, riding camels, and having the time of our lives. Then he put me back on the plane, waved, and sent me home. I didn't see him again for another nine months.

That was my dad.

Thinking of him settled my nerves. I leaned my head against the airplane pillow and dozed off.

CHAPTER 19

Tap, tap, tap. I cracked one eye open to see a finger sticking in my shoulder repeatedly.

"Pasha. Stop."

He pushed himself past me and sat in the empty chair to my right. I looked down at my watch. I'd only been asleep an hour. But I was groggy, and it took me a few seconds to realize where I was. I remembered the events of the previous day, hoping somehow I was locked in a bizarre but increasingly realistic dream.

I tried closing my eyes again but Pasha was persistent. "You really don't have to do that, you know."

"I think that I do," Pasha said. "You are going back asleep."

"I don't know what happens in your country," I said, turning away from him, "but in America, people like to go to sleep when it's dark. Even on airplanes."

"I have been mulling this over and over in my head," he said, ignoring my sarcasm. "The information I gleaned from the website. The names, the articles, the pictures, the theories. The Shroud of Turin. The cloth Jesus Christ was supposed to be buried in. I read and I read and I read. All of this research, devoted to this one artifact, centuries old, and quite possibly a fake. Some of their research, some of the theories, they are fascinating. These people who studied this, they are really into it."

"How so?" I asked.

"They have dedicated a big part of their lives to this so-called shroud of Turin. And when you read all of it together..."

"What?"

"I don't know if I can put it to words. It's like...it was more than just an information sharing website."

I looked at him blankly. "I'm not sure what that is supposed to mean."

"Looking at the entries and the dates, there was more and more activity over the last month. It was building and building, messages flying back and forth. These people were in more and more of a hurry. Something was going on."

"Like a deadline or something, a time constraint they had to meet?" I offered.

"Yes. Exactly," Pasha said. "Deadline."

I thought about this for a minute. "Do you think they knew it was going to be stolen?"

"From reading these materials, I think they clearly would have liked to get their hands on this shroud."

"What do you mean, Pasha?"

"I will try to explain in a way you will understand," Pasha said.

"Well me and my G.E.D. appreciate that very much," I said, as he looked at me blankly. As usual, he was fully unaware of his condescension.

"There is an enormous amount of material related to textile testing. One particular person who had access to the site, Maggie Duncan, seems to be a cloth and textiles expert of some sort. There are pages and pages of chemical formulas and regulations for inspecting such an artifact."

"They stole it so they could look at it." I said this almost to myself, trying the idea out loud to see if it fit.

Pasha nodded slowly. "But why would they do that?"

"Maybe they didn't have access to it, they couldn't get at it any other way. Maybe in their quest for scientific truth they became over-zealous. The shroud is only seen once every twenty-five years. Did you know that? The rest of the time what is visible to the average human being visiting Turin is a replica, a fake. The powers that be in the Roman Catholic Church, well….let's just say they are apparently very protective of this thing."

"How do you know so much?" Pasha asked.

"I dated a shroud expert once," I said. "Remember?"

Pasha nodded. "Dah, dah."

"So unless they were hand-picked by the Vatican, who are very selective with who even gets to lay eyes on this cloth, they would never get a chance to see it in person. They'd have to wait for the next world tour, just like the rest of us."

Pasha nodded. "Which would be when?"

"It went on display in 1998. So 2023 is the next time it is available."

"That is long time, Matt," Pasha said.

"Too long for someone so eager to wait," I agreed, rubbing my eye. "So, say they stole it. Now, that in and of itself was quite a caper to pull off. Did you read about the theft? They had explosives, they were in, they were out. These people knew exactly what they were looking for and they didn't mess around. Four small-charge C-2 explosives were placed at just the right spot, in the exact area underneath the shroud. They were detonated, and the burial cloth of Jesus fell through the floor. The case that it's in lands right in front of them and methodically, these people proceed to cut the glass, suction it off, and swipe the shroud." I lean toward Pasha. "And they didn't leave one fingerprint."

I leaned back in my seat and took a sip of diet coke. "Do you honestly think a group of scientists, whose lives are about research, theories, artifacts, and digging things out of the dirt could pull off a stunt like that?"

Pasha searched for an answer. "Perhaps they had help."

"Yes," I said. "Here's what I think. The scientists want to get the shroud in their greedy little scientist hands. They want to touch it, they want to test it, they want to study it, they want to do whatever it is that scientists do with it. They get impatient. Maybe they make requests to the Vatican to see this artifact and are rebuffed. So they decide to take matters into their own hands."

Pasha nodded as if he understood this logic. "Did I tell you about my uncle? He is former KGB. Lives in Moscow. He is now Russian mafia."

I blink. "Your uncle is in the mafia? And what does that have to do with this?"

"Yes," Pasha said, unaware that this was a tidbit of highly interesting information. "He is in mafia. So when they want something done that is not quite legal—"

"Which is often, if he's in the mafia," I interrupt.

"Yes, often," Pasha said. "Anyway, they have people to go to. These people can do certain things, or get certain things, for my uncle. When it is something he does not want to do himself, he can call a few friends and make it happen."

"So maybe these scientists have some friends in high places," I said.

"My uncle says that good people are hard to find." He added, "And expensive."

"I wonder how much something like that operation would cost, assuming you could find the right people to do it?" I asked. "How much does it cost someone to steal the Shroud of Turin?"

"Yes, Matt," Pasha said, "this is my point. Why do they go to such effort to steal something that is an artifact? Something that many people say is a fake anyway. Why is it worth that much to them?"

I rested my chin in the palm of my hand and considered this. If these people stole it, this was the question. Why would they do it? Why would they hire someone to steal it for them?

A more daunting question was behind that. If they did steal it, they had it in their possession somewhere. Of course the police and the Vatican would be interested in recovering it. It was a part of church history and an invaluable artifact with cultural, and religious significance.

But who would kill somebody over it?

Daniela was dead. My gut said she was dead because of the shroud. Someone, somewhere, wanted her gone because of it.

Lots of questions. Questions I wanted to ask someone. And that someone happened to be in London.

Larry Beckham.

"I don't know, Pasha. But that's why we're taking this little trip."

I leaned my head back and closed my eyes again.

I just hope we can find Larry before someone else does.

CHAPTER 20

I had been through Heathrow Airport one time, again with my father, when I was thirteen. We were on our way to Moscow and had a few hours to kill. The only thing I really remember was the people. The sheer volume of people was amazing, and that coming from a kid who had spent a lot of time in New York City.

Today was no different. As we sat at the Starbuck's and drank chai lattes and ate scones, we could not help but be entranced by the number of people milling by in front of us, a sea of bodies that appeared interconnected, moving in the same direction and at the same pace. Hoffman reminded us it was the busiest international airport in the world. Most were on their morning commutes, rushing to catch their flights and make their connections. If you told me I was in John F. Kennedy I would have believed you. The people looked the same, a myriad of colors and nationalities, ants marching down the terminal.

It was 8:45 in the morning, so we waited until 10:00, and then hailed a taxi outside the terminal.

"Harrod's Department Store, please," Hoffman told the cabbie as we squeezed into the small car.

Even though the plan was to stay just long enough to get face-to-face with Larry Beckham at Cambridge, Hoffman insisted we be dressed for the occasion. Looking at the three of us, I could understand his point. I was wearing raggedy jeans and a white Carolina t-shirt. Pasha had on sweat pants and a t-shirt. Hoff had the obligatory fraternity khakis and blue button down. Classic Chapel Hill slob chic. We were a ragtag crew. Of course, we hadn't really had a chance to pack, with our unwelcomed house guest showing up.

I had a sneaking suspicion Hoffman also wanted to stick it to his father. If that meant a shopping spree at his expense, I was happy to help out.

We dropped three thousand dollars that morning in less than thirty minutes.

We walked in looking like we didn't know where our next meal was coming from. But we emerged looking like we were headed to the next photo shoot for GQ.

"We should stay in London for awhile," Hoffman said. "Three Americans—well, two Americans and a Rooski—all dressed up? We could take this town over."

"Before you get too excited," I said, "let's just remember what we're here for. We need to find this guy Beckham and see if we can figure out what kind of connection there is to Daniela's death."

"I know, I know," Hoff said. "But you don't have to be so serious all the time. Geez. I'm funding this endeavor, remember. I should get to have some say in our itinerary."

He smiled, waving his dad's credit card in front of my face.

Pasha grabbed the card, looking at the people milling about on the street outside the department store. "You should stop waving this around, you American idiot. It is like you are asking someone to come up and take it."

"Okay, okay," Hoffman took the card and put it back in his wallet. "Let's go find another cab."

It was a simple plan, really. Head to the University of Cambridge, which was about fifty miles outside of London, look our friend up, and ask him some questions. It seemed like it would be easy. Kind of like any interview I would conduct for a newspaper article. I was confident that soon we would get to the bottom of this. Confident we made the right decision to come to London and see for ourselves what Mr. Beckham had to do with the shroud, the website, and Daniela. He would be able to give us the answers we needed.

Confidence is an interesting thing. Sometimes it's good. It can lead you to places you wouldn't normally go, where fear normally stops you. Other times, though, it's like putting on a pair of dark sunglasses in an already smoky room. It causes you to miss some obvious things. If I was older, more experienced, or less naïve, maybe I would have realized we were falling into the second option.

CHAPTER 21

We hailed another taxi with no trouble and meandered through a spider web of roads which eventually led northeast. Soon we were past the buildings, hotels, and factories, and pushing through the lush, green countryside. Rain sporadically fell, glistening, enhancing the beauty of the hills and valleys.

Within the hour we were pulling into the town of Cambridge, a town northeast of London. We knew we were close to the fabled university when we saw students milling around everywhere. The school dominated the scenery of the community, unlike universities in larger cities, where the school is merely a subtlety in the urban landscape.

"Kind of reminds me of Chapel Hill," I said as we drove around the perimeter of the campus.

I was struck by the sheer beauty of the buildings themselves. They seemed to have been sitting there for centuries, and maybe they had, for all I knew. The campus in Chapel Hill was like an exhibition of the various architectural influences of the fifties, sixties, and awful seventies all tangled together. A large, stately brick structure with huge windows, placed beside a building made out of concrete with tall, thin anti-riot glass. I was told once these were built so students wouldn't be able to throw a chair through the window. In case they didn't like their grades, I guess.

Students hurried to classes across massive grass lawns, while some strolled along the walkways, or sat in the open quads eating lunch, listening to their iPods.

The taxi driver let us out in front of what appeared to be the main quad, a lush green space in-between two large old brick lecture halls. Hoff slipped him some cash and he sped off.

"This feels way too familiar," Hoffman said, staring at a group of co-eds with backpacks on.

"What are you talking about?" I said, slapping him on the shoulder. "You never went to class."

"I didn't say I went to class," he said. "But I did hang outside of the classrooms a lot."

"Hilarious," Pasha said. "Why don't we use our energy to focus and try to find this Larry Beckham person?"

"Good idea. Let's find someone who can point us to the religion department," I said. "That's where we're going to find his office."

After stopping a few students, who were clueless, we found a helpful guy who pointed us toward the Sykes Building, the center for religious studies. He stared at us briefly before asking us where we were from.

"North Carolina," I said. "We just got here for orientation."

He smiled. "Studying abroad, I take it?"

I nodded. "That's the plan. Thank you for your help." We headed across the quad before he could ask any more questions.

Everything was falling into place. Now we needed to find Beckham and discover what he knew about Daniela's death and the shroud's disappearance. And if he proved to be a good guy, we would warn him to watch his back.

We bounded up the stairs of the Sykes Building. Inside we found a registry on the wall of the professors and their offices.

"There he is. Beckham, Room 115," I said as I pointed at the sign. I glanced at Hoffman and Pasha. "Let's go see if the professor is ready for visiting hours."

We took the stairs down to the first level and walked along a narrow hallway of offices. Up ahead, around an office door, a group of students had gathered. They were huddled together close, speaking in hushed tones. One tall boy was comforting a girl as she cried on his shoulder.

A cold sense of sickness crept around the edges of my stomach. Something wasn't right.

As we drew closer, we watched the room numbers tick by as we passed an office. Above the door where the students were gathered was a placard:

Dr. Larry Beckham 115
Religious Studies

Pasha, Hoffman, and I looked at each other for a few seconds, not saying a word. But I was certain I knew what they were thinking. We weren't going to get a chance to talk to the professor, Daniela's associate. There would be no interview with him, no insight into his relationship with Portonova. We were too late to warn him of impending danger.

It was just yesterday that Becklar79 caught me in the shroud site chat room using Daniela's name.

Now I had the awful feeling Professor Larry Beckham was dead.

Nauseated, I approached the students standing there, reminding myself that we were supposed to be exchange students.

"Hi there," I said, as innocently as possible, to a tall blonde slumping underneath the weight of her book bag. I motioned to my two fellow students. "We were supposed to meet with Professor Beckham today. Did something happen?"

"You haven't heard?" she said. And then, in starts and stops, "Professor Beckham…died…late last night. Apparently he was coming home from a class and lost control of his car. He was found down an embankment close to his home, about twenty meters from the road. It looks as if…as if the car lost control, spun around several times, and hit a tree. He…passed instantly, they think." She wiped her eyes with her sleeve.

Even though I knew it was coming, it hit me like a blow to the abdomen. I pinched the bridge of my nose and gathered myself.

"Do they know…I mean, do they think it was an accident?" I asked, trying not to sound too suspicious.

"I don't know," she said. "I don't think another car was involved or anything like that. It's so sad. He was such a great professor. Everybody loved him."

I was hungry for details. "What class did you have with him?"

"Religions of the Ancient Near East," she said, a glimmer of a smile across her face. "He was so passionate about it all. He loved ancient religions and knew so much."

"If you don't mind my asking, did he ever talk about the Shroud of Turin?" I knew I was pushing my luck but I figured an innocent question couldn't hurt. I quickly added, "It's just that it's a pet interest of mine. I knew he had an interest as well. We wanted to…talk to him about it."

She nodded and her eyes met mine. "Actually, yes, he did. He loved to discuss the shroud and the mystery behind it. In fact, it seemed like he discussed it more and more lately. He would get so excited. And then, of course, it was stolen. This sent him into the stratosphere."

I tilted my head. "What do you mean?"

"Well, he couldn't stop talking about it. Last week he spoke about the shroud every day in class. Talking about its significance to the world, the theories of how it just may be real. He would always say that one day the world would know the secret of the shroud."

"The secret?" I raised my eyebrows, but again tried to temper my curiosity. Casually, I pushed ahead. "What does that mean?"

She shrugged her shoulders. "I have no idea. I took it to mean he believed the Shroud of Turin was much more powerful of an artifact than people have made it out to be. That there was something significant behind it we have missed."

"Interesting," I said, trying to play it cool. "Guess he thought he was onto something there."

"Yes," she wiped her eyes again. "But I guess we'll never know, will we?"

I had pushed enough.

"I'm sorry for your loss. I'm sure he was a great professor. A great person. I'm sorry we didn't get a chance to meet him."

She muttered a thank you and re-joined her friends in their hushed conversation around his door. The door, I noticed, was taped off, much like Daniela's, with crime scene investigation tape. I assumed it was locked.

It would be a bad idea to try to get into his office, I told myself as Pasha, Hoff, and I walked away. A very, very stupid, foolish, not to mention irresponsible idea. I reminded myself discretion is the better part of valor and I was in a foreign country that did not take kindly to foreigners breaking laws.

This conversation was going on in one side of my brain, while the other side was trying to figure out how we were going to get in that place and find out what he knew about Daniela, or the shroud, or perhaps both.

CHAPTER 22

"So he's dead too," Hoffman said to no one in particular as we walked through the heavy double-doors and into the English sunshine.

"It was bad idea to come here," Pasha said. He couldn't stand still, so he paced around on the pavement outside. "A very bad idea. I don't want to get shot, or get our car to blow up, too."

Hoff leaned back against a fence post, pulled out a pack of cigarettes and lit one. He took a long drag, the way he did sometimes on our porch back home when he was letting things settle in his mind. My own head was spinning, trying to let this latest piece of information sink in.

"Maybe he really did have an accident," Hoffman offered half-heartedly. "Some kind of freak coincidence that has nothing to do with Portonova."

I could tell he didn't believe it. I sure didn't. I kicked at a clump of grass.

"Come on, Hoff," I said. "Really? Put it together. If I had to bet, I would guess the same person is responsible for both of these deaths."

"So what?" Pasha said. "Who cares? It is time for us to start to mind our own business. We have gone too far as it is. Why should we care about how this man died, if it was accident or not, and who might have killed him?"

"Because someone needs to figure this out," I blurted out, with more emotion than I intended. It surprised even me, and I took a breath, trying to settle down. "And maybe no one else can but us right now."

Pasha looked at Hoffman for sympathy. "Can you believe what Matthew is saying?"

Hoffman puffed on his cigarette and didn't say anything. His eyes met Pasha's but glanced back down to the brick sidewalk.

"Okay," Pasha said, nodding. "So you are on his side, I see? Two against one, is that how it is going to be? You are two stupid, stupid Americans who are going to get you and your Kazakh friend's brains blown out."

He threw his hands up in the air and walked away, muttering something in Russian I was pretty sure included more than a few expletives.

Hoff and I watched him walk away, talking out loud to himself, shaking his head.

"He'll come around." Hoffman put his arm around my shoulder.

"Hey, listen, I'm going to see this thing through," I said. "But I don't want to drag you and him along with me if you really don't want to be here. This is already dangerous enough. Two people are dead. We've been chased by a man with a gun. It might get worse before it gets better. If you guys need to go back to Chapel Hill tonight, you should go. I'm choosing to be here but I don't want to make your choices for you."

He slapped me on the shoulder hard. "Don't insult me, man. I am not just along for the ride here. I told you I'm in this with you all the way."

I nodded my thanks, feeling the emotions swell inside again, afraid if I opened my mouth I might lose it.

"Don't worry about Pasha. He'll be alright in a few minutes. He just needs to work it out in his head, take a few deep breaths. And maybe a few shots of Russian vodka." He looked at me out of the corner of his eye. "So what now, Detective? What's the next step?"

I cleared my throat. "We need to get into that office. We need to find out what he knew about Daniela and the shroud."

"I was afraid you were going to say that," Hoffman said, dropping his cigarette, extinguishing it on the ground with his foot. "Well, we better have a great plan, because I really don't want to call my dad from Cellblock One of a

London jail, not after we racked up three thousand dollars in credit card expenses at Harrod's."

"Don't worry," I said with a smile. "I have an idea."

CHAPTER 23

Dr. Larry Beckham's secretary, Mrs. Louisa Farnsworth, was in a tizzy. She must have been in her late fifties, with streaked gray hair wound so tightly into a bun that it made her eyes look like they were dragged slightly out of place. As I stuck my head in her office, she was flitting around from one corner of the cramped space to the other, and had a phone with a long cord wrapped all the way around her. She had obviously been talking on the phone while she was searching for something in the office. Littered across her desk was a mound of paperwork, a couple of old coffee mugs, a ring of keys and a two-foot high stack of three-ring binders. She was violently scanning the desk and the bookshelves for some hidden document she could not locate, and, with each paper shuffle, her voice grew more and more exasperated. It was clear the events of the past twenty-four hours had sent her into a tailspin.

She finally saw me and waved me in as she tried to wind down her phone call. We politely stepped inside the mayhem and stood with our backs up against the wall beside the door. I was quickly reconsidering my great plan and felt the sudden urge to bail when she slammed down the phone, gathered herself for a moment, sat slowly, and said in a rich English accent, "Can I help you?"

I paused for a few seconds. Pasha kicked my shin with his foot.

I cleared my throat. "Mrs. Farnsworth, we are exchange students from the United States. We wanted to say how saddened we are by the loss of a great professor."

"Yes," she said, "well. It has saddened us all." With that, she grabbed a tissue off of her desk and blew her nose with a goose-like honking sound. I knew if I looked at Hoffman or Pasha at that moment I would lose it. Out of the corner of my eye I could see both of them forcing themselves to stare at their shoes, not each other or me, and certainly not Mrs. Farnsworth.

"What can I do for you gentlemen?"

"We also came by," I nodded at my fellow students, "because we were supposed to meet with Professor Beckham today."

At this she frowned, and began another frantic search through her desk to find her calendar. She excavated it from the bottom.

"Your names?" she said.

"Matthew Harkin," I said, immediately wondering if I should have given her my real name or not.

"I don't see you on his calendar, Mr. Harkin," she looked at me over the top of her glasses. "Not that it matters at this point."

Hoffman spoke up. "You made the appointment through email, right Matt? So maybe it never made it onto your calendar."

"That's right," I ventured. "We have an interest in the Shroud of Turin, and the professor was going to share some insight and his latest findings with us. I know this is probably not the best time, but we were wondering if we could, well, have access to any of his shroud materials that he was going to show us today? Maybe we could just peek in his office to see if there was anything he was preparing for us?" As soon as I asked the question I knew it was a mistake. The man just died last night, for goodness sake. Here I am, asking to get into the man's office, for research materials. What was I, some kind of research freak that I had to have it now? "It's for research for another seminar we are taking."

She stared at us over her glasses again without saying a word, this time for what seemed like a full minute. Finally she removed her glasses and rubbed both of her temples.

"Gentlemen, even if I had time to let you into his office, which I don't, you couldn't get in anyway. The police have marked it to be searched, and no one is allowed in or out. Now if you come back by next week, when things have settled down, maybe I will be able to help you. But until then—" she stood "—good day."

I knew a protest would not be wise, so we nodded our condolences again and filed quietly out of the office.

"Sorry guys," I said as we walked down the hallway, "I thought we had a shot. Guess I was wrong."

We walked outside, and Hoffman was grinning from ear to ear. "Good thing you brought me along on this adventure, fellas." He pulled his hand out of his jacket pocket and produced a large ring of keys.

"You swiped those from Mrs. Farnsworth? Are you crazy?" I said. But I had to admit, I was impressed. "How did you do that?"

"One summer, I begged my dad for one-on-one magic lessons," Hoffman shrugged. "And he said I'd never use them…"

Pasha gave him a high five.

"We'll have to send your father a thank you note for that, too," I said. "Now listen, guys—we can't hold onto these keys for long. Time to act fast."

CHAPTER 24

Nightfall came quickly and we headed back to the professor's building, intent on getting in and out of there quickly. We were on edge, and I had to do a little convincing to get Pasha back there with us. He came, even though he was muttering about getting arrested, dumb Americans, and how they did it back in the mother land.

I had some experience breaking and entering into professors' offices now, and this time I was more confident. I couldn't get Daniela off of my mind; I was motivated. I wanted to know what Beckham knew, and I wanted to know why he was dead now too. I wasn't buying for a minute he had a single-car accident. Neither were Pasha and Hoffman. There were pieces of a larger puzzle I was confident we would find if I could just spend a few minutes in his office.

We waited until the hallway had been clear for a full five minutes, and we knew no one had noticed us loitering. The plan was simple. Pasha would wait outside with a book bag, playing the role of student if anyone happened to come by. Hoffman and I would quickly search the office, looking for anything related to the shroud of Turin, Portonova, the website, or anything else that looked suspicious.

One problem was the sheer number of keys on the key ring. We had ruled out a few, based on size and shape. It still left about twenty keys that were possibilities. I focused on the door, trying key after key as fast as I could.

"Come on, Matthew," Hoff whispered, an urgency creeping into his voice. "Move it along now."

I felt a bead of sweat form on my forehead, growing with each key that didn't work. "I'm working on it."

I was down to the second to last key when I slid it into the door and turned it. The door popped open.

"See, no problem," I said, grinning at Hoffman as we stole into the office.

Thankfully there were no windows and it was a relatively small space, so we could turn the light on without worrying. Pasha closed the door behind us, hopefully replacing the yellow police tape across the door as planned. We heard his soft steps move a few yards down the hallway, where he was to position himself by the water fountain.

The desk was covered in strewn papers and books. The bookshelves were stacked with large, dusty tomes, file folders everywhere, and various artifacts in every imaginable corner. I breathed out a sigh as I surveyed the room.

"The old professor wasn't what we would call organized, was he?" Hoffman said, staring at the mess. "I'm not sure, but you could make a case that Secretary Farnsworth was not doing her job."

"We have to move fast," I said, picking up a disorganized stack of papers.

"I realize that, Matt, but what exactly are we looking for?"

The truth was, I didn't know. How would I know what to look for? I was no expert on the Shroud of Turin or middle eastern archaeology. The closest I had come was watching Raiders of the Lost Ark as a kid with my dad. I felt myself start to panic.

"I don't know, Hoff. Just look around!"

We started to scramble. There was no telling how long we had and I wanted to get out of there fast. I scanned the bookshelves while Hoffman sifted through the desk.

"It's like a needle in a haystack," I heard him mumble, "except we don't know what the needle looks like."

Papers were flying off of the table behind me but we had no time to be neat. I scanned through the bookshelves for anything related to the shroud of Turin. I found a series of research books devoted to the shroud. I leafed through each of them but found nothing. No notes, nothing personal written. There had to be something else here. But in our quick scan we were coming up empty.

A knock came at the door. Hoffman and I froze, waiting.

"You two need to be finished now!" Pasha said in a forced whisper.

We began to move again, ignoring Pasha as we frantically searched the office. Prospects were growing dim. We needed to get out.

"There are two girls out here," Pasha said again, a little louder. "I don't know what to do!"

"I got nothing," Hoffman finally said, throwing his hands up.

"Me neither," I said. One last time I fumbled through his desk. In the top left side drawer I rummaged through a pile of papers, pens, sticky notes, reaching toward the back of the drawer this time. I pulled out a black checkbook. Almost without thinking, I opened it up, grabbed the check registry, and stuffed it into my pocket. We had to go and I was grasping at nothing but straws.

Reluctantly, we turned the lights off and opened the door. I came nose to nose with a very worried, slightly hyperventilating Pasha, uttering Russian profanities to himself and me.

"Oh," I said, "were you waiting for us?"

I slapped him on the back as he rolled his eyes. No one was coming down the hallway so we quickly re-taped the door.

"Let's get out of here guys. Who's hungry?"

Hoffman smiled. "Now that's what I'm talking about. We passed about a dozen pubs on the way here."

He led the charge down the hallway.

"Time to sample some night life."

CHAPTER 25

Mugg's Pub was down an alley a few blocks from the campus. We holed up in a back corner booth and ordered some drinks. I hadn't been the stereotypical college beer drinker—I couldn't stand the stuff my friends drank, the cheaper the better. I did, however, enjoy a good quality import every once in a while.

"Try to order an import here and see what happens," Hoffman said.

"They'd bring me a Bud," I grinned. "No thanks. The smell of that stuff reminds me of a few blurry, ugly nights in high school I'd rather not remember."

"My friends and I used to pay premium dollar for Budweiser," Pasha said. "It was status symbol to drink American beer in Russia. No one wanted to admit it tasted like it came from rotten well in the back of my house."

Our drinks arrived and we ordered fish and chips. I brought out the check register I had quickly nabbed, and began leafing through it.

"Lots of checks going out, and he recorded deposits going in as well. They must not use debit cards much around here. Looks like he paid for everything with a check. This looks like a grocery store, quite a few to some kind of bookstore, gasoline expenses, the usual stuff."

"How about deposits?" Pasha offered.

"Paycheck deposit is listed. He apparently got paid pretty well. Not much else in that category," I said, scanning it. "Wait a second. Wonder what this is?"

I held it up closer to make sure I could read the scrawled handwriting right.

"Looks like a deposit made into his account six months ago for $25,000. And look who it's from."

Hoffman was busy downing his black and tan, but grabbed the register and studied it. "Theophilus? Who is that?"

"Theophilus? He is one of the names that appeared on the website," Pasha said. "We don't know anything about him other than that."

"And now we know that he paid the good professor a nice sum of money," I said, taking a slow sip of my beer. "Wonder why?"

"Take it from me, okay," Hoffman said, "people can owe money for all kinds of reasons. Friends of my dad, they are always paying each other for something. Usually it's related to gambling. This one dude got whipped by my dad so bad on the golf course that he carried it over into a poker game the next night."

"What happened?" Pasha asked.

"The guy ended up writing a check to my father for $53,000," he smiled. "He used it to buy my boat."

The waitress brought a basket of chips and I grabbed a few, my brain churning with this new information.

"There is a lot that it could be, you're right, Hoff. My best guess, though, is this Theophilus person paid him for some kind of services rendered."

"I thought you guys said these website guys were working together? Now you're saying one of them is paying another one?" Hoffman asked. "I'm not sure that makes sense."

"Maybe Theophilus is the only one paying anyone," I ventured. "Quite possibly, Theophilus is the ring leader. The one who is calling the shots. So Larry Beckham did work for Theophilus, related to the Shroud of Turin. Theophilus pays him. The shroud is stolen. And now, Beckham is dead."

Pasha spoke up. "Sounds like we need to find Theophilus."

I nodded. "I agree. But that could prove to be difficult. He didn't leave us much of a trace of his whereabouts on the website, did he?"

"Dah," he said. "Nothing."

"We do, however, know where someone else from that site is." Pasha took a long pull on his beer before speaking again. Finally, he said, "Yes. We were able to isolate a name with a shipping address I found while digging around behind the site. Once you get the name, it's really not all that hard to find them."

"Margie Duncan," I said. "The Textile Queen."

CHAPTER 26

Benito dialed the number Father Paniti had given him, to use only if absolutely necessary. As much as he did not want to call, since he had been unsuccessful in his assignment so far, he knew he needed to phone in. His employer would want a full accounting.

He had waited at the airport exit for four hours. There was only one way in and one way out and he assumed, for a while, they were waiting for him to tire and leave. He could be patient when it was necessary. Biding his time along the side of the road, he watched intently as car after car filed out. No white Jeep emerged.

After waiting until sunlight cracked through the darkness in the sky, he decided to drive through the airport parking lots. He drove slowly through thirteen of them until he found the car, parked, backed in against the concrete wall. They had carefully picked a space where the bullet hole wouldn't be easily noticed.

Benito grimaced at this, wondering if they had perhaps rented a car and escaped. Or they were still here. Or…he heard the scream of a jet engine above him but dismissed the idea. Perhaps they were inside, talking to the police, or waiting in a terminal. A public place would be a fine spot to hide.

He strolled through the two terminals, checking every conceivable corner as discreetly as possible. The next flights did not leave for another two hours, but there had been some arrivals and he was not the only one there. He checked the baggage claim areas last, and then walked out.

That's when he made the call to Father Paniti.

"Benito." The older man's gruff voice answered, not with the serene cadence that Benito had grown so accustomed to. It was staccato and tight and he knew this would not be a pleasant conversation.

"You have lost them, my son." Father Paniti paused and sighed loudly.

A shudder came over Benito, with a feeling so foreign to him that his feet skated across the parking lot as if on ice, his head dropping at the Priest's leaden words. It was shame, and it crashed down on him like a wave from a childhood ocean.

He was going to try to fake it and buy more time, but obviously the Father knew more about the situation than Benito had suspected. Denial would only cause more problems now.

"Yes," Benito said. "I found them at their house, but they escaped."

"Are you not the professional, Benito?" the Father barked. "And they are the amateurs, no?"

"Yes," Benito said, barely above a whisper.

"Then how could you let them get away?" The Father's voice was filled with anger and distress.

"I will..." Benito cleared his throat. "I will find them, Father. Do not worry."

Paniti laughed darkly and his voice grew quickly distant. "Do not worry. Yes, do not worry. About tomorrow. For today has enough trouble of its own. But if we do not worry about today, Benito, then what becomes of tomorrow? Nothing. We are no more. All hope is lost."

Benito did not know what to make of the Father's words. He tried to reassure him. "I will get them, Father. I will finish this job for you, if it's the last thing I do."

"Yes, yes," Father mused, his voice growing soothing once more. "You are not done yet, my son. There is yet still time. The three boys have come to England. They seem to know more than we ever imagined. The woman professor must have given her boyfriend some information. They came to see the second on our list, but fortunately he was dealt with by another associate in London before they could speak."

Benito took it in. How could Father Paniti know all of this? He learned long ago to never ask too many questions about the job at hand. Keep it simple. The target, the method, the plan. The payment. Move on. Now, though, he wondered. How would the good priest know flight information? It would seem that he was better connected than he let on. "What do we do now?"

"Forget England. Fly as quickly as you can to Edinburgh. We must act quickly to neutralize the third target."

"But what of the boys?" Benito asked.

Father Paniti chuckled again. "God is with us, my son. They are a surprisingly resourceful bunch. And because of that, I believe you might have a chance for a reunion with them when you arrive."

Benito hung up the phone, grabbed his bag from the car, and headed back to the terminal. The urgency and forcefulness of the Father's voice had shaken him.

He was not going to fail him again.

CHAPTER 27

The myriad of checkpoints one had to pass through to enter the inner bowels of the Vatican was stunning. Father Paniti avoided the place as much as possible. Once, a long time ago, he was smitten by the grandeur, its sheer importance to the world, the solemnity of it all. It still impressed him, he was not ashamed to admit. How could it not, being what it was? He had once roamed these halls with secret pride, basking in his own self-importance. In them he had met some of the most sincere, humble, spiritual men he would ever know. They challenged him with their piety, encouraging him to go to greater and greater lengths in his commitment to God and his fellow man.

He had also met some of the most cunning, loyal men he had ever encountered. Men of aspiration, ambition. And of great, secret knowledge.

His footsteps echoed loudly in the cavernous, intricately-etched hallway. There was no pride in him now. No pompous air. Eventually he had tired of that, realizing its futility and the shallowness it had brought to his life.

Cardinal Montenegro had recognized Paniti's commitment and intelligence. And his loyalty to the Church. He had brought him along slowly, carefully, cautiously. More responsibility here, another tidbit of information there, testing him, probing him, for any sign of weakness.

He and the others eventually agreed that, yes, Paniti would make a fine candidate.

Paniti had been groomed for his role here, to be a part of Il Protettorato. He knew that now; he wasn't as naïve as he had once been. He appreciated the attention he got from certain men in interesting and sometimes powerful positions within these walls.

Some days he wished he could give it all back. To go back to working with clean hands and pure heart. To a place where he was ignorant of certain realities. Such thoughts were foolishness, though. Foolish when there was so much work to be done. When so much was at stake.

Immense men for immense pressures, the Cardinal was fond of saying. Never before had he felt the weight of those words so squarely on his shoulders.

Paniti tried to breathe evenly, moving his slowly failing body through two sets of large, ornate double doors. He stole quietly down a passageway and turned left, two more rights, and left again. There were doors everywhere, leading to antechambers, small offices, retreats for solitude. Some of them were only accessible to a certain few. As old as these halls were, there was an enormous level of security and technology behind the crumbling stones and bricks. He had no doubt he was being watched by multiple cameras and multiple security guards, though no cameras could be seen.

He found the door he was looking for. A centuries-old, simple wooden door, with an iron knocker in the middle. He drew it up slowly, and gave it three firm raps. A red beam of light appeared from a hidden place in the door. He stared ahead, holding still. When the retinal scan was complete, the door latch unlocked and he made his way into the room.

CHAPTER 28

The other members of Il Protettorato were already present, though Paniti was greeted with stone cold silence. He sat in the only tall chair that was empty, waiting for the meeting to be called to order. Looking slowly around the room, he surveyed the faces of the other eleven members and wondered if he looked as old and worn-down as they did. Whether they would admit it or not, the singular task they had devoted their lives to had taken its toll on each of them. They each had on a hooded, brown robe, tattered from many years of this secret service to the church. The frugality of their garb belied the positions of authority each of these men held. They held vast power both within and outside of the Church. Billions of dollars in assets were under their control. Seemingly endless resources to fight the good fight. And yet, here they were, in a situation that none of them envisioned. Their faces were long, old, creased and cracked, laced with frowns.

Being the sole source of protection for the One True Church was not for the faint of heart, after all.

Cardinal Montenegro finally spoke, breaking the thick silence, bringing the meeting to order.

"Father Paniti," his carefully enunciated words echoed off the walls of the small room. Montenegro's words were few, slow, and sure. He had the knack of speaking so it always seemed that it was only after great thought and deliberation. "Give us the report."

Paniti smiled thinly. They already knew the report. He knew they were aware of the situation and the critical nature. What other reason would they have been convened in an emergency session?

But he obliged the cardinal. "A month ago the shroud was stolen in the middle of the night by thieves—"

"Not just thieves!" interrupted one of the members. "We know this, Paniti. Do not give them such credit.

Thieves want money. What this person wants is…altogether different."

Paniti nodded. Everyone understood the gravity of the situation. "A rogue group took the shroud. It is gone, and our efforts to get it back have not been rewarded. Yet."

The cardinal spoke again. "The police, as you know, have been of very little help in this matter. We have had to resort to other means to give us what we need. Father Paniti's efforts here have so far proven to be quite unfruitful."

Paniti bristled but remained calm. "We have men in the field, pursuing all leads. Our technology division has proven very resourceful and directed us to the website of the individuals under suspicion. From this, we generated leads, which we are in the process of eliminating. I have confidence the Membership will find that very soon we will have rid ourselves of these…wayward souls…and will have the shroud in our possession again. It is true, my operative in the United States found some unexpected complications after he eliminated target number one," Paniti crossed his legs and breathed evenly. "I have no doubt, though, this is a mere hiccup and will not distract us from our mission."

"Three outsiders are now very close to us, Paniti!" the same member said. "They are snooping around and are putting us all at risk. Putting the Church at risk!"

Paniti sighed. "Soon, brothers, these three students will no longer be a concern."

"This is becoming expensive for us, brothers," Montenegro said. "And risky. But I still have full confidence in our brother here that he can handle this responsibility."

He turned to look Paniti in the eye. "Should he not, however, his service to this Membership will not be needed any longer. The assets he lives off will be folded back into the accounts."

He smiled at Paniti, the charisma that had allowed him to rise to such a position dripping from his lips. "We know you can do this, Brother Paniti. We are counting on you. The future is at stake. Get this done."

With that, Paniti was dismissed. He hurried away. Even for a man of his age and stature, he was shaken.

CHAPTER 29

The largest textile museum in the world, for those interested in such things, exists in Aberdeen, Scotland, of all places. The centuries-old University of Aberdeen sits on the windblown, northeastern shore of the country, exposed to elements that distinctively shape the countryside. Any existing vegetation grows close to the sandy base. The sand itself is moved and removed constantly, providing an ever-changing landscape to the keen observer.

The Historical Museum of Textile Arts sits inside the Marischal Building on the campus of the University. The buildings here are gothic and spired and evoke the awe one feels knowing that centuries of students and faculty have studied and dedicated themselves to the discipline of asking questions and seeking answers. The Marischal Building's sharp architecture sits like a pointed granite spider, appearing even taller than it's actual height. It is a cathedral, evoking thoughts and feelings of the spiritual. This, even though it is meant for celebrating the higher power of the mind, not devoted to worship of God or religion.

Inside the Marischal building, on the eastern side of the campus, the textile museum eventually found its home. Its founder, Professor Margaret Duncan, was a tenured faculty member of twenty-six years, had nursed the museum along, first in the basement of the sciences building in what amounted to a broom closet, then upstairs to a larger room. Her notoriety had grown, not only within Scottish academia but also in the international world, as an expert in ancient linens, cloths, and textile techniques. In this realm she had no equal. A dynamo on the speaking circuit, she had been featured on American television shows with investigative reporters like Geraldo several times, assisting with tomb explorations or mummy excavations. She even became something of an

113

international expert witness, called to testify at various trials.

It could be said that without Margie Duncan there would not be much of a University of Aberdeen. Certainly without her the museum she had so carefully crafted, the school would not have the prominent position it now held. It occupied two floors and a basement in the dramatic building, operated with one full-time and two part-time staff, and was one of the crown jewels of the campus. When Professor Duncan was not traveling internationally, or instructing in the classroom, she was deep within the recesses of the museum archives, sorting, testing, and analyzing to her heart's content. That was her first love, and all of the fame and fortune the world could offer to her was no match to a few solitary hours of research.

It was in this coastal, Scottish town that Hoffman, Pasha, and I found ourselves. The three of us hadn't spoken much after getting onto the small commuter jet in London and heading to Aberdeen. I, for one, felt the increasing urge to forge ahead and find out the answers. Pulled in this direction, almost. Something just ahead that beckoned and yet stayed just out of reach. And my friends, well, they hadn't bailed on me yet.

Could I stop myself if I wanted to? The question had crossed my mind. I was not sure of the answer.

I considered what little we knew about Margaret Duncan. She was a contributor to Larry Beckham's website, and was apparently an associate of Daniela's. According to Pasha, who had done the most perusing of the website files and had researched her online, she was brilliant, well-respected in the academy, and more important to us, had written frequently about the Shroud of Turin. Interestingly, it appeared that just in the last year or so had she altered her view on the shroud and now supported a much earlier dating of the cloth. A dating that would put it around the first century.

She had discovered something.

This was why we were here, after all. This was why it was so important now to get to her and talk. To hear what she had to say, and try to connect the dots from the Shroud to Scotland and London, and back to Chapel Hill. To Daniela Portonova.

There seemed to also be a larger agent gripping the three of us now, though. This ancient artifact had risen from the grave and was dancing and alive in front of us, drawing us in. Its power lay in the possibility that it brought forth. I was a realist, a truth-seeker, just like my father. He ingrained in me a hard-nosed drive for facts, a questioning and often cynical mind. He had little time for religion. My mother, however, had a deeply spiritual side. She was private about it, but would take me to the Episcopal church in Manhattan on occasion.

As I stood in front of the Marischal Building and took in its enormity I remembered that spired structure from my past and the thought of my mother raced through my heart. I suddenly felt very far away from home.

Hoffman crushed his cigarette under his feet and brushed his shaggy mane out of his eyes. "Alright, boys, here we are. I swear I've spent more time on campus in the last two days than I ever did when I was a college student myself. I used to avoid professors, not look for them. But I guess it's time to go find another one and see if we can put an end to this."

Pasha was pacing and he had grown quiet. All he gave us was a hushed "Dah." He was nervous, but there was no reason for me to draw attention to it.

We went through the tall, scrolled double doors that led us into a granite-floored lobby. There was a small reception desk, which no one happened to be monitoring at the moment. Our eyes were automatically drawn upward, to a ceiling that was the palette for a weathering, highly detailed fresco. Below this painting hung a series of tapestries from the ancient wooden beams that ran across the length of the building. Five of them were on display in front of us, each one impressive in its own right. My eyes moved to the one in the middle. It was an intricate portrait of a scene outside the tomb of Jesus. I could make out two women and a man. One of the women I remembered to be Mary. I wasn't sure of the other one . The man was clearly the risen Christ. He was strong but compassionate, looking down at his two subjects with a serene smile. What caught my eye was behind him, in the empty cave. On a slab of rock just inside, there was what appeared to be a neatly folded cloth. The burial shroud of Jesus.

Margie Duncan had certainly placed that as the centerpiece of this room. I imagined that for someone like her, the shroud of Turin was like the holy grail for a Crusader, or landing on the moon for an astronaut. It was the ultimate prize. The opportunity to study it only came to those at the top of their fields who had dedicated a lifetime of years to their craft. It's importance to her rang out clearly in the tapestry above.

I was busy staring at it and didn't notice the young woman who emerged through a doorway behind us.

"That is professor Duncan's piece de resistance," she said, startling the three of us. We must have jumped, because she took a step back and eyed us carefully. "Pardon me, I didn't mean to surprise you."

Her Scottish accent pierced the quiet, open room. She pushed her red, disheveled hair out of her face, revealing piercing green eyes.

I tried to play it off. "We were just admiring the tapestry."

She glanced up at it with us. "It's probably from the early tenth century. A Scottish nobleman recovered it at the end of the Crusades and it was kept in his family's private collection until professor Duncan convinced him to give it to the museum. It is renowned for it's craftsmanship, the quality with which it has been preserved and, of course, the detailed image of the shroud of Christ."

I glanced at Pasha and Hoffman, who were staring at her and not the tapestry. They were mesmerized by her accented voice. I shot them a look that said, *calm down, boys.*

"You gentlemen aren't from around here, are you?" she said, smiling.

"What makes you say that?" I said, in my best southern accent.

"Lucky guess," she laughed. Turning to the tapestry again, "There was the overriding sentiment in those days that the one who possessed the shroud of Christ would hold unknowable powers. It was highly sought after by many, many men."

"Do you think that's true?" I asked.

"About the powers? It is the stuff of legend," she said, brushing my question aside.

"What do you think about its recent theft?" I said, perhaps too aggressively. Hoffman eyed me fiercely but bit his tongue.

She retreated. "Thieves will be thieves. Probably sold on the black market and long gone at this point." Moving behind her desk, she assumed her official responsibilities now.

"What can I help you with?" she said, all business.

I cleared my throat. "We're exchange students, traveling from Oxford. Here to see the museum, and perhaps the Professor herself?"

"You're in luck. She just finished giving a tour a few minutes ago. I imagine she is still downstairs, in the dungeon."

Behind us a group of about two dozen students were walking back up the steps and out of the facility.

Worry flashed across Pasha's face. "Did you say dungeon?"

Her smile reappeared. "That's what we call our basement. It feels like a dungeon sometimes. Cold, damp, underground. Don't be scared, nothing will hurt you down there."

117

Hoffman, Pasha, and I glanced quickly at each other.

"Thanks," we all said together, and headed toward the stairwell to the right.

CHAPTER 30

The upper two levels of the museum were spotlessly organized and uncluttered; the clutter had obviously found its way downstairs. Row upon row of long, dusty shelves met us at the bottom of the steps. They reminded me of the stacks in the old Wilson library on the Carolina campus. When I really needed to clamp down on a research paper or study for an exam I would find one of the hidden desks in the stacks and knew that I may not see anyone else for hours. I still did it occasionally now, when I needed a quiet place to write an article.

"Geez, this place smells," Hoffman complained, holding his nose. Pasha sneezed.

"A lot of dust in here," I said, picking up an old shirt folded on the shelf in front of me. "It looks like some ancient garage sale. Nothing like four-hundred year old clothes to get your allergies going."

There were rolls of material scattered around the place, rugs labeled from Turkey, Pakistan, and Egypt. Boxes on top of boxes of who-knew-what seemed to have been left to sort through at a later date.

Stopping to listen for a minute, I heard nothing. We began walking down the long rows, which must have been nine feet high in some places.

"Professor Duncan?" I called out. No answer.

"Should I go back and see if she's upstairs?" Pasha offered. He was getting more than a little freaked out down here. A quick look back at his pallid face confirmed it.

Before Hoffman or I could respond, we heard a faint whooshing sound. Followed by a thud.

I put my fingers to my lips and motioned for them to stay right behind me. We crept down the long, musty stack and I peered around the edge, down a long hallway.

Halfway down, a lumpy form lay on the floor. My heart thumped loudly in my chest, but I forced myself to

119

move toward the shape, leaning down over the crumpled body.

"Looks like we found Professor Duncan."

"Look at her neck, guys," Hoffman said. There was a dark red line around her throat. Blood oozed from the wound and onto the floor. A small puddle of it sat at the back of her neck, growing by the second.

"She was strangled," I said, "and I'm no crime scene investigator, but I think we heard her fall a few seconds ago. Which means…"

We glanced at each other, knowing what it meant. The killer was still close by.

No sooner had he said that than something whizzed by my ear and exploded into a wooden beam set vertically along the wall, sending splinters everywhere.

"Get down!" I shouted, ducking while pushing Hoffman and Pasha as hard as I could down the aisle. The three of us crashed into each other and scampered along the floor. Pasha was moving along on his knees. Hoffman dove in-between two of the tall wooden stacks. Instinctively, we went in different directions. I squirmed the other way, quickly, and then sat up with my back against a bookshelf. Everything was quiet again. No movement. I breathed in deeply, trying to get my heart to slow down and stop pounding in my ears so I could hear. No footsteps. Maybe the killer was waiting. I glanced over and realized I was close enough to Professor Duncan to touch her. The dark red pool had grown and if I stayed here much longer it would be at my shoe. Queasy, I told myself this would not be an appropriate time to lose my lunch.

A distant exit sign caught my attention. There was an arrow pointing to the right, the direction Hoffman and Pasha had gone. I waited a few seconds longer and still heard nothing. Maybe the murderer was calmly waiting us out at the exit door. Or stalking us quietly down the rows until he picked us off, one by one. Either way, I couldn't stay here any longer.

I moved, as close to the ground as possible, along the wall. Across from me were shelves that held long bolts of fabrics.

Whoosh. Whoosh. Whoosh.

I heard the quiet footsteps along the carpeted floor and I froze. Was that Pasha or Hoffman? Or the killer? When I stopped, they stopped as well. If my friends were still in here, they were being awfully quiet. I forcibly pushed away the thought that the killer had already gotten to them.

Focusing my eyes ahead, I made myself move, regardless of what lay ahead. Quickly now, I edged down the wall and turned right just before the last set of stacks, and entered a dark corridor between two tall shelves of what looked like giant rolls of fabric and rugs that must have covered the floors of ancient castles. I looked to my left as I crept along, trying to peer through and see if I was close to the exit door. That was my mistake.

I didn't see the man wheel around in front of me until it was too late. He brought the end of his gun down across my forehead, rattling my skull and knocking me to the ground. I lay there on the carpet, feeling the blood rush to my head. In my grogginess and pain, I was somehow still conscious. I looked up and saw my attacker, slender build with platinum blond hair. I knew instantly he was the same figure we had escaped in Chapel Hill. The same one we'd seen on the cliff, putting a bullet in Daniela Portonova's head.

He grabbed a handful of my hair and yanked me up, then threw me back down on my stomach. His foot glanced across my ribs, the force flipping me on my back.

I spat and wheezed. "You must have been pissed...when we got on that plane." This earned me another kick, this time glancing off the shoulder. I never was good at keeping my mouth shut.

"Where are your friends?" he stood over me, brandishing the weapon. It was the first time I had heard the tall, thin man speak and I noticed a thick accent. Italian, for sure.

I tried to smile. "I don't know what you're talking about. I came here alone."

He was quickly in my face, shoving the warm end of the barrel of the gun against my temple. His teeth were dark yellow, three of them almost black, but it was his eyes that got to me. They were cold and dark—but steady.

"I can get you the name of a good dentist in Italy," I said. "No one should have to live like that."

He raised the butt of the gun again, when a crash came from down the corridor. One aisle over, something had smashed into the ground. I cursed Pasha and Hoffman under my breath for being careless.

The man pushed me back to the ground and motioned for me to stay put. He kept his gun trained on me but was quietly moving down the corridor, listening.

Just then another noise, the sound of glass breaking, toward the exit door. He turned with his gun and fired three times through the shelving, hoping to connect with an unseen target.

In that moment, I saw what he did not. The tall, heavy stack behind him was moving. Rather, someone was moving it. He turned just in time to see the old, wooden shelf, ten feet wide and loaded with heavy fabrics, come crashing down on top of him.

It hit him squarely, the full force of its weight driving him into the ground. I heard a sick, crunching sound and knew bones had been broken. His gun flew out of his hand across the carpet, toward me. He wasn't moving, either unconscious or dead. I didn't want to wait around to find out which.

Pasha stood hunched over on the other side of the fallen stack, clutching his knees and breathing deeply.

Hoffman emerged from the other row, quietly fist-pumping, celebrating our escape.

I grabbed the gun and shoved it in my pocket. I would dump it in the first garbage can I saw.

We did what our first instincts told us to do. We bolted out of the back exit door of the basement, up the exterior concrete steps, and walked as fast as we could, without drawing attention to ourselves, to our rental car.

CHAPTER 31

Hoff hung up the phone and slid it back into his pocket. "I told the girl at the front desk to call the police, and not to go downstairs until they get there. Wish we could have stuck around, but I don't think that would have been a very good idea."

The proximity of a dead body and a violent encounter with an assailant trying to kill us with a gun had put me in a state of shock, triggering memories from my childhood.

Grainy footage of another murder was looping through my mind. My father, sitting in a chair, in black and white. His face beaten and bruised, his head hanging down. Two hooded men standing over him with assault rifles. Another standing closer to the camera, railing against the United States and their presence in the Middle East.

The memories of that day were always fresh in my mind. The CIA shocked us when they knocked loudly on the door of our Upper West side apartment and escorted us to their New York headquarters. We were given no information, only that it was urgent, and about my father. My mother, sister, and I rode quietly in the back of a black Suburban, each of us developing our own personal scenario of the worst case in our minds.

We drove into an underground parking deck and were whisked up an elevator, into a large situation room. There were men and women frantically working there, in front of large monitors, many of them on phones, having animated conversations. The tension was palpable. The agents led us out of the elevator and through the large room toward a smaller conference room in the back. One of the images etched in my mind is that of my mother, head held high, walking in front of us. She was a stunning, beautiful woman, and no more so than that day. The activity in the room ceased as eyes were drawn to us, mainly to her. It grew awkwardly silent. A few men stood, acknowledging our presence. My mother nervously nodded at them, trying to hold it together. We didn't know it then, but they were paying their respects. They knew what was about to happen.

We huddled in the room with the head of the New York division and they briefed us on the events. Dad had been kidnapped by a radical terrorist organization and was being held hostage. Their demands were the usual, including the release of several known terrorists in United States custody and the removal of troops from the region.

The director at this point peered over his glasses and said with as much sympathy as he could muster, "As you know, Mrs. Harkin, it is U.S. policy not to negotiate with terrorists."

Mom nodded quietly. They showed us the latest video released by the news network Al—Jazeera; we were in frantic tears.

We spent the rest of that day and into the night in that room. A staff assistant brought in a plate of food no one touched. We were waiting for something, anything, to happen. No one, not the CIA, not the military, no operatives in the area, had any idea where he was being held. They knew only that he was in a secure location somewhere in North Africa. The video had been poured over by experts who declared it authentic but found nothing to determine his location.

So we waited, knowing the next information we would receive would likely not be good.

At 1:06 in the morning, another video was released. A gun was pointed at the side of his head. It was then we heard Buddy Harkin's last words.

"Matthew, Meredith, I love you so much. Be strong, be strong for your mother, okay?" he said, and somehow managed to smile and wink. "Sandra, my heart will always beat for you. I love you with all my heart..."

The gun went off and it jolted all of us from our seats. He slumped over in his chair and the screen went blank.

Al—Jazeera had just shown the murder of my father on international television.

I ran from the room without knowing where I was going. Just away. I took off down a hallway and sat down in a corner, wedged between the wall and a soda machine. Burying my face in my hands, I wept. For my father, for my mother. For my sister and me.

Mom found me eventually and we huddled on the cold floor together, holding one another tightly for a long, long time.

I sat in the rental car, staring through the window at the stark buildings we passed by, my mind moving from that memory to another place.

"God, we don't talk a lot," I thought to myself. "I don't try to talk to you at all, really. Especially after what happened to dad. I don't even know if you're really there. But if you are, well, we could use some help about now."

I shrugged, leaning my head back on the seat and closing my eyes.

CHAPTER 32

We found a café in a shop-filled section of Aberdeen and holed up. Pasha discovered we had two hours to kill before the next commuter jet back to Heathrow; he made us reservations online. Hoff located an automatic teller machine down the block and took out enough euros to last us for a while. The police would find Duncan's body soon, and the consensus among us was that the quicker we could get out of town, the better. No one wanted to get stuck in Aberdeen, Scotland, so that the Scottish authorities could treat us to an extended vacation. Having just gone through a crime scene investigation a few weeks ago, we each knew how intense and time-consuming it could be. The other, bigger reality, however, was that none of us felt safe at this point unless we were on the move.

There were a lot of students at the café and it helped us feel relatively secure. Hoffman got us some soft drinks and food and we sat down at the corner table.

"Did this guy chase us?" Pasha said. "How do we end up halfway around the world, being chased by the same guy?"

"He was after the professor," I said, trying to sort through the recent events. "Think about the course of things. The shroud is stolen. Then people start to lose their lives. Daniela. Then Beckham in London. And now, Duncan."

"And almost us," Hoffman offered. I nodded.

"All of these people were deeply involved in research having to do with this religious relic, the shroud. There were five people, five names we gleaned off of this website, right Pasha?"

"Yes," he nodded. "That is correct."

"Three of them are now dead. Two of them are left."

"Actually, fellas, we don't know if the other two are dead or alive," Hoffman reminded us.

"That's right," I agreed.

127

"So this man was just coming after the professor," said Pasha, "and we happened to get in the way?"

I tugged on my lip for a few seconds. "I'm guessing he was coming after her. But he knew there was a good chance we'd be there, too. Maybe he even knew we were in Scotland, coming after Duncan as well. He kills her before we get a chance to talk, and then he almost gets a two-for-one by getting rid of us at the same time."

"Except that now he's buried under a pile of rugs," Hoffman said. "So nothing else to worry about, right?"

I sipped on my diet coke. "I wish it were over, Hoff. But I've been going over the timing of these things, and it doesn't add up. Considering our chase with him and the fact that we got on that plane and immediately came to London to see Professor Beckham, it just doesn't work out."

"You mean," Pasha said, "he didn't kill Beckham."

"Exactly. Someone else did."

Hoffman nodded slowly now, no smile on his face any more. "He has a partner."

"Yep," I said. "My guess is, he has partners, plural. Or more likely, he is working for someone. A hired gun. With other hired guns out there."

"It just doesn't make sense," Hoff erupted, his emotions finally breaking through his cool veneer. "What is the point? Why would they want to kill all of the people associated with this website?"

"They were onto something," I said.

"Onto something. Okay," he muttered. "Like what?"

"What if they figured out that the shroud was really, you know, the shroud?" I offered.

"Meaning the real cloth that covered the face of Christ?" said Pasha.

"So what if it is?" Hoffman challenged. "What's the big deal? Put it in a museum somewhere, sell tickets, do whatever. It's ancient history."

"Well, its disappearance set these killings off."

"You are thinking the website group stole it, and some people are now after them? They want it back?" Pasha said.

"*The Catholic Church is ticked off and wants its stuff back,*" Hoffman said in his best movie trailer voice, chuckling.

I thought about this. "Maybe," I said. "It would explain some things. But does that really make sense? Why wouldn't they simply rely on the proper channels, on the authorities, to find the missing shroud? If it's just a case of recovering a lost artifact, some stolen property, wouldn't they do the normal things? Police search, investigation, rewards, the usual?"

"According to my internet research, those investigations are underway and have been for some time," Pasha replied.

"That's what doesn't make sense to me," I offered. "Why would they instigate an investigation, and then potentially undermine it by hiring other agents to go after these people?"

Hoffman chimed in. "Not to be too insensitive to you, Matt, but think about the way these people have died. Does it seem like they wanted to try to recover the shroud from Portonova, or the other two here?"

"To me," Pasha said, "these look more like assassinations. And remember, my uncle has had some experience with this kind of work in Russian mafia."

I thought about this. "Planned killings." That made sense. They didn't intend to try to kidnap these people, hold them for ransom, make them take them to the hidden shroud, anything like that. These professors were targeted and then mercilessly murdered.

"So why would you send someone to kill these people?" Hoffman asked. It was the big question, it seemed, and we let it hover over the table for a few minutes. The answer was simple, really. There was only one reason they would go to this extreme.

"They knew something, something big, something that has the power to impact important people in the Church, or the entire Church itself. Something so dangerous it made more sense to try to have them killed than to let this secret out," I said.

"But what is it that would cause them to react so forcefully, so aggressively, that they would end lives because of it?" Pasha said.

I thought back to the handful of religion classes I had taken. "Things like this have happened before, you know. Think about the Crusades, the Spanish Inquisition. Think about all of the atrocities that have been done in the name of God and religion. History says that when the Church is mortally threatened, certain people within it react forcefully and decisively."

Pasha's face darkened. "I don't think you can throw the whole Church together into one big pot, Matthew. I have members of my family who are good people and very loyal to the church."

I nodded. "Chances are it's like anything else. There are a bunch of well-meaning, good people there, but a few bad seeds."

"But back to the question," Hoffman said, "what kind of threat does a two-thousand-year old piece of cloth pose to the Catholic Church?"

"I don't know," I said. "But you can't deny there is something to this. Something more underneath the surface here."

No protest from Hoffman or Pasha.

"Pasha," I said, "who's left?"

He nodded, glancing down at his open laptop. "Theophilus. We don't have any data I can glean from the website. He is a ghost right now. And salva316. I tracked him down using a couple of research techniques I developed a few years—"

"Pasha," I interrupted, "just spare us the details and tell us who it is."

"Andrea Salvatore. He is a world-renowned archaeology expert."

"Where is he?"

"Italy. In-between Milan and Turin."

"But how do we know he's actually there?" Hoffman asked. It was a good question.

"Let me have your cell phone," I said to him, reaching my hand across the table. "Pasha, can you find a phone number?"

Pasha clicked away at the keyboard again. "Nothing personal for him, if that's what you mean. I did find the website of an organization he seems to preside over. The Archaeological Religious Institute of Italy. In Turin." He glanced up at me. "There's a contact number here."

I got the number, punched in the digits, and took a deep breath. An Italian female voice answered.

"Yes, do you speak English?"

"Un momento," she said.

"Yes?" came another woman's voice a minute later.

"Hello, my name is Matthew Harkin," I said, in my most professional voice. "I am calling on behalf of the Archaeology Department at the University of North Carolina at Chapel Hill. We are hosting an Archaeology Conference next year and we wanted to inquire about the possibility of Dr. Andrea Salvatore speaking at this engagement. Is he available?"

"Dr. Salvatore is not here," she said.

"Ah, I see," I said. "Is he traveling, or will you be talking with him soon?"

"It is a good question," she said, hesitating. And then, "We do not know where he is. He has not come into his office here today. Or yesterday." She seemed flustered. "I have had two other people inquiring as to his whereabouts."

"Today?" I blurted out.

She paused. "Yes, of course, today, though it is no business of yours I am sure. When he comes in I can take a number and have him call you."

"Oh, that won't be necessary," I said, wondering who else might be looking for Salvatore. I pushed a little further. "Do you think he is in town now?"

"Yes, he is at his home in Biella, as far as we know," she said. "We hope to see him soon and will let him know you called."

"Do you have a home telephone number for him?" I was really pushing my luck now.

"Good day, Mr. Harkin," she said, and hung up.

"Good day," I said to the dial tone. I shared the conversation with Pasha and Hoffman. We speculated who might be looking for Salvatore besides us. By the time we could get there, it might be too late. Just like with the others. The longer we sat here, the more time we were wasting.

"Pasha, book us a different flight," I said. "How's your Italian, guys?"

We made sure there was no one watching us as we exited the café. With our heads down and our coat collars pulled up around our necks, we found the car and headed, once again, to the airport.

CHAPTER 33

The flight to Milan, Italy was full. The air conditioning on the plane was not working. We were separated from each other, as we had booked the flight last minute; we were lucky to have somewhere to sit at all. Hoffman somehow ended up with a window seat in the back. He had his sunglasses on and was either staring out the window or sleeping, I couldn't tell. Pasha had made out the worst. He was stuck between a large woman with a loud Texan accent and an even larger Italian man, who bore a striking resemblance to Super Mario. Both of them spilled out of their seats, sweating, and squeezing Pasha from both sides. He looked at me, helpless, and rolled his eyes. I gave him an animated thumbs-up and turned back in my seat to try to catch some sleep.

Leaving the crime scene worried me, and as I finally got a chance to sit down, I ran through the worst-case scenarios. What if there were cameras? What if we left fingerprints? I swallowed hard and thought of another, even more serious issue. What if they thought *we* were the murderers? The girl at the front desk could probably describe each of us fairly well, even if they didn't have photographs. Surely they would find the bald assassin and link him with forensics to Duncan's murdered body. But they would also realize someone else had been down there?

And what if the assassin wasn't dead, and had made it out? This thought gave me another wave of stress, and I tried to sit back in the chair and relax. He would come after us again. *What is done is done*, I told myself. *When we finish this we can work it out with the police.* Maybe that was naïve, but I convinced myself that all we could do now was focus on what was in front of us.

Finding Andrea Salvatore before the killer did.

Deep inside me, though, something told me Hoffman was right. For all we knew, they had already found and killed Salvatore and this Theophilus person, whoever he or she was. Maybe they had dozens of assassins out there. Who knew? The truth was we had no idea who we were dealing with. And the further along we went with this crazy chase, the deeper we were getting in over our heads.

I closed my eyes, trying to settle down, but I was scared. I thought about my dad. What would he say? I wished so badly he was here in the chair beside me. He would tell me exactly what to do. He would be able to handle something like this.

"When you are doing what you think is right, never, ever give in. No matter who or what is in your way."

The words rose from some reservoir deep within, of memories stored away. My father had said it when he was home from the Middle East, after a particularly grueling month of imbedded reporting with troops during Operation Desert Storm. He coined the term "imbedded" during that assignment and thrilled the country with his reports from the front lines.

"I was imbedded before imbedded was cool," I could hear him say. No one wanted him there. Not the military, not the government officials, not even many in his own news agency. He went anyway, talking his way in, befriending the right military personnel, bribing a few. Whatever it took. That was his attitude.

So when I asked him why he did it, that's what he said.

"When you are doing what you think is right… "

I felt resolve blooming in me again, thinking about him. I made up my mind that whatever happened next, I would pursue the truth. Wherever it led. The truth about Daniela Portonova's death. And the truth about the mysterious Shroud of Turin.

When we finally landed and passed through customs, we found a place for Pasha to connect his laptop. We knew Salvatore lived in a town called Biella, about eighty miles from Milan and forty or so from Turin.

Pasha typed in Portonova's URL, but this time, the site didn't come up. Instead, the page said "Explorer can't open the page".

"Someone's taken the site down," Pasha said, leaning back in his chair and folding his arms.

"What does that mean?" Hoff said.

"I was hoping to glean more information about salva316 here," Pasha explained. "But now that is impossible."

Pasha hammered away on the keyboard again. "On a different note," he said, turning the computer toward us, "they found Duncan."

We huddled around the computer monitor. The headline screamed "Famed Professor Found Savagely Murdered – Murderer On the Loose". The details so far were scant, but it was clear they had found her and evidence of the scuffle in the basement. They did not report finding another body. An investigation was ongoing. They were pursuing multiple leads at this point.

"He escaped," Hoffman said quietly, like someone had punched him in the stomach.

Pasha's eyes were wide. "Which means they are going to keep coming after us."

I was determined, though, to keep things positive. "There's nothing we can do about either of those things right now. When we get back to the United States, we will talk to the authorities and tell them everything we know. Right now, though, we need to keep moving. So, what *do* we know, guys? We have a name and a location, right?" Anything to keep us focused and moving in the right direction.

"Yes," Pasha said, "we do."

"Then let's get going," I grabbed my bag and rose from the table. "Besides, how many Salvatores in Biella Italy can there be?"

Hoffman and Pasha looked at me and rolled their eyes simultaneously. I chose to ignore them.

"Let's go. We don't have all day."

"Geez, take it easy, will you?" said Hoff. But he saw that my resolve, and he had no choice but to grab his stuff and along with Pasha, trail behind me to the rental car stand.

CHAPTER 34

We piled into a late-model Audi and I managed to guide us out of Milan, with Hoffman buried in the map we bought at the airport, calling out directions. What little we saw of Milan was beautiful and I made a mental note to come back sometime and see the city. But this was not exactly a sightseeing vacation.

"I can't believe we are at Milan and we're driving away," Hoffman complained. "Don't you guys know that this is the fashion capital of the world? Do you know what that means?"

Pasha blankly stared back at him.

"That it's the model capital of the world too! Models, European models, as far as the eye can see." Hoffman sulked. "And we're driving away from the place. Brilliant, guys. Just brilliant."

"It's okay," I said, patting Hoffman on the knee for good measure. "Daddy will take you there sometime if you just ask."

Hoffman stared out the window. "Daddy's not going to be taking me anywhere for awhile after he sees this credit card bill we're racking up. We can only hope he doesn't cancel the card before our little road trip is over."

I tried to keep my eyes on the road, but the Italian roadside was enticing. Beautiful stretches of highway, mountains on one side and deep, lush valleys on the other. Intricate Mediterranean homes dotted the landscape. Vineyards were everywhere. The Audi was cruising and I shifted gears often along the curvy roadway, feeling the power and control underneath me. My mind was elsewhere, though. Basically, trying to figure out what we were going to do when we got to Biella.

The road signs we passed told us we were almost there. Following an arrow that pointed us toward the mountains, we took an even curvier road, and started to notice elements of a town ahead.

"Now what?" Pasha said. For once, I didn't have an answer.

Hoffman pointed ahead. "Stop up here. Pull over."

"Right here?" I asked.

"Just do it, Harkin," he barked. I obliged, and parked in front of some kind of local vegetable stand. Hoffman jumped out and ran past it.

"Where is he going?" Pasha asked. I watched him and then I realized what he was doing.

"Of course," I said, smiling. "He's getting the phone book."

Hoffman opened up the doors to the oldest phone booth I had ever seen, went inside, and emerged with something stuffed under his shirt, his head swiveling around, until he got back to the car.

I was skeptical. "Hoff, do you honestly think that a guy like Salvatore, probably the most famous resident of this town, would have his name listed in the—"

"Here it is!" Hoffman said, holding the phone book in my face for good measure. "Salvatore, Andrea. There's only one. Right here in the white pages." He looked up at me and smirked. "And I thought you were some kind of investigative reporter."

I tried to ignore his comment. "What's the address?"

"Via Degiovanni 12."

"That on the map?" I asked. He looked for a few minutes and shook his head.

"Let me have that," I said, grabbing the floppy paper. I hopped out of the car and walked around behind the vegetable stand. A young man packing tomatoes in bags looked up at me and said something in Italian. I assumed it was something to the effect of "can I help you?"

"We are lost and need directions," I said, slowly and for some reason overly loud. It wasn't like he was hard of hearing just because he spoke a different language.

He looked at me like I had an extra ear growing out of my head.

"Via Degiovanni?" I said.

Now we started getting somewhere. Taking the map from my hands, he laid it out on the table in front of us and emphatically pointed to where we were now. Then he traced a route on the map, with a couple of turns, and landed on an area that had no streets. He took a pencil out of his shirt pocket and placed a star on the spot.

I thanked him and he continued to stare at me. I wasn't sure what he wanted until I picked up a bag of tomatoes and he started nodding and smiling.

When I got back to the car I tossed Pasha the sack of vegetables.

"Got a snack for you guys," I said, and we were off.

CHAPTER 35

After several wrong turns, we found Via Degiovanni. The street sign was practically invisible from the road, covered by vines no one had taken the time to trim. It looked like the kind of community that didn't get a lot of visitors. People here probably had little use for things like street signs.

We turned down a road so narrow the right side of the car was almost touching a craggy mountain, shooting vertically into the sky. On our left, a steep drop-off left us with the width of one decent American highway lane for the gravel road. It was slow going as we hugged the mountainside in turn after turn. Gratefully we started to see houses. The homes were larger than the ones we passed through town, and much newer. Clearly people living on this road had money and they wanted to escape the crowds. Why else would you build on the side of a mountain?

We passed eleven homes, and the gravel road abruptly ended, feeding into a paved driveway. A mailbox sat outside marked with the number twelve. As we headed around the final curve, the house came into plain view. It was large, three story pastel and peach-colored home, with a low-pitched, red roof, the mountain behind it, facing an unimpeded view of the lush, green valley below.

"Must be some good money in archaeology these days," commented Hoffman.

There was a three-car garage on the side of the house that was closed, and no cars in the driveway outside. We parked in front of the garage.

"Are we just going to walk right up and knock on the door?" asked Pasha. It was a good question, actually. How should we approach this? And what were we going to find when we entered the house? At this point we were prepared for anything. The conversation with the lady on the phone reverberated in my head. They had not heard from him in a day, at least, and they seemed concerned. Maybe not concerned enough to come to his house and look for him. Yet.

Which meant salva316 was possibly gone. Or possibly dead.

"Well, fellas, I don't want to sneak around and have him think we're trying to, you know—"

"Whack him?" Hoffman helpfully suggested.

"Exactly."

"The front door it is, then," Hoff said. We hopped out of the car.

Taking in a deep breath of fresh Italian air, I climbed the granite steps with Hoffman and Pasha at my heels. With each step my stomach sank further. I hoped we had caught him in time, but more and more I felt like we were going to be too late. Again.

One way to find out.

I pushed the ornately decorated doorbell and heard deep chimes ring throughout the house. We waited. No footsteps coming to the door, no answer.

Three more times I rang. No response.

I looked past the house to the left, then back where we came, down the road. No houses were visible from here, and I saw no one who watching us.

"Let's have a look around," I suggested. We walked around to the garage side again, and peered into the windows. There were three spaces there, and two were empty. The third was occupied by a small, sporty looking car.

"One car is here," I said.

Hoffman whistled. "One sweet car, dudes. That's a brand new Ferrari 612 Scaglietti."

"Are you sure?" I said.

"My dad has one in his garage. No one is allowed to even breathe on it," he shrugged. "It's kind of his baby."

There was a side-entry door beside the garage and I tried the handle. It was locked.

141

"We can't just walk in," Pasha said, nervously pacing. "We're probably already internationally wanted after what happened this morning. Do you want the Italian police to arrest us now?"

"Take it easy, Pasha," I said. "Just trying to find the good doctor."

I continued walking around to the back of the house. There was a small swimming pool and a Jacuzzi tub with a stone patio. A large set of French doors opened up onto the patio and, beside it, a door I guessed went into the kitchen. I tried the kitchen door, but it was locked too. I stood there for a minute, thinking. I knelt down, sliding my hand under the doormat. No key.

"Nice try, detective," Hoffman whispered.

I then ran my hand up above the door, stretching to the top as I reached a small brick outcropping. Sliding my hand down it, I felt something. Jackpot. A lone key, sitting on top of the last brick.

Waving it at them and grinning, I placed it in the lock and turned the key.

The door opened into a spacious kitchen. Food-caked dishes filled both sides of the sink as well as the smaller sink on the granite-topped island. A good sign, I thought. Someone was still here. Albeit someone who didn't like to clean.

"Where's the maid?" Hoffman whispered, eyeing the mess.

It was a beautiful house but the place was a wreck. Newspapers littered the kitchen table, and books. Hoffman picked up a book. It was on archaeology, written in German. Beside it, another tome in English. A laptop was sitting on the table as well, next to an old bowl of milk-soaked cereal.

I cleared my throat. "Dr. Salvatore?" I waited for an answer. Nothing.

"Dr. Salvatore? Are you here? Are you okay?"

Still no response.

Each of us called his name out as we explored the house. Nothing.

I walked through the living area, equally messy, when suddenly I felt movement behind me. I whirled around, mental visions coming to life of the blonde man with a gun trained on me.

Instead, a brown cat meowed and brushed by my leg.

"Whoa!"

I took a deep breath, and Pasha and Hoffman rushed in from the adjacent room.

"Just the cat," I said. At least the cat was still alive. That had to count for something.

"Nothing downstairs, Matt. The lower level is empty."

We headed up the stairs, cautiously. There were three levels, and the second appeared to be a living area with four rooms that surrounded the staircase. Slowly we checked each room. They were almost identical. As unkempt as the first level was, the second was surprisingly neat. Each room included a bed, dresser, and bathroom off to the side. We looked through the rooms, under beds, in closets, in the bathrooms. Still nothing. No sign of Dr. Salvatore.

"I'd say the good Dr. Salvatore doesn't spend much time on the second floor," Hoffman said.

We climbed the steps up to the third floor. A white door was at the top of the staircase, closed. We looked at each other, as if to say, who is going first? Pasha and Hoffman graciously took a step back and allowed me to go first.

"Thanks, guys," I whispered, and turned the handle. It opened up into one large room, and it was immediately evident this was where Salvatore spent most of his time. It was a museum. There were three large desks in the center of the expanse, covered with maps, papers, and thick research books. Two long walls were bookshelves that stretched from floor to ceiling, with a ladder system that rolled along the wall to retrieve books unreachable from the ground.

Pasha whistled. "There must be a thousand books here."

The other two walls were like an archaeologist's trophy case. Artifacts covered the walls, hanging and on shelves, or standing on the ground. Stone tablets with ancient engraving. A giant oar most likely from a Viking vessel hanging on the wall. A full suit of armor. Beside it, a sarcophagus that looked like it was straight out of King Tut's tomb. And hundreds of other items from around the world.

But no Andrea Salvatore.

"I hate to say it, guys, but our friend isn't here," Hoffman finally said, staring at the artifacts in the room.

We trudged back downstairs to the kitchen. I walked through the great room, with a large fireplace in the middle. Hoff and Pasha had already checked it out. Where was this guy? Maybe they had gotten him already. Thrown him off the cliff, buried him in the woods. It was possible, too, that he was gone, in hiding somewhere. Whatever the case, it was starting to become clear this could be the end of our road.

In front of me was a mural. It was striking, encompassing the entire wall. As I thought about our journey, I stood and soaked it in. A painting of the Italian countryside. A boy tending cattle. Further ahead in the valley, a vineyard. It met the Mediterranean, a vast blue expanse reflecting the sun back onto the landscape. Then something caught my eye. In the middle of the mural, I saw a fine line going up, then cutting across and back down again, a rectangular shape. It almost looked like a small door.

I walked closer. Maybe it *was* a door. Reaching out, I gave it a light push.

"Guys, you need to come see this," I called out.

An opening had been built into the mural on the wall. Barely visible, certainly not to the casual observer. Beyond the door was a small set of steps that led down, into the dark.

"A secret passageway?" Hoffman said, looking over my shoulder. "Sweet."

"We're not going down there, are we?" asked Pasha.

A string hung down in front of me and I pulled it, turning on a single light bulb overhead. It lit up the stairway, which curved around to the floor below.

"Dr. Salvatore?" I called out again. "Are you down here?"

I listened intently. All I heard was the drip-drip-dripping of a leaky pipe. We started down, each step creaking loudly. Turning the corner of the steps, there was a light switch on the left, which I turned on. Then we realized where we were. Racks and racks of wine were scattered around, like a maze. The walls were solid rock, and had been cut out to form a basement wine cellar. We walked through row after row of bottles.

"I think he has more wine bottles down here than books upstairs," whispered Hoffman. I nodded. He probably wasn't too far off base, judging from what I saw.

Suddenly we heard a shout from behind us and the three of us spun around.

"Hold it right there! Don't move one more muscle!"

There was a gun pointed at us, three feet away, shaking uncontrollably. Holding that gun, arms locked, with two hands, was a wild-eyed man with electrified hair. He was one big ball of frenetic motion. I wondered how his trigger finger was doing.

We had our hands raised, and he simply stared at us, shaking. Either he was waiting for one of us to make a move, or trying to decide what he should do with his three new prisoners.

I slowly put my hands out in front of me, which caused him to train the gun directly at my head.

"Are you...Dr. Salvatore?" I asked.

He kept the gun pointed at me and didn't respond. Clearly he was unsure of his next step.

"We're looking for Dr. Salvatore," I tried again. "Is that you?"

Again, no response. He just kept staring holes in us with those eyes.

"We're here to help," I said, putting my hands all the way down. "We wanted to see if you were still alive."

This caught his attention. He finally spoke.

"Of course I am alive. And why wouldn't I be?"

I exhaled for the first time in a few minutes. "My name is Matt Harkin. These are my friends, Hoffman, and Pasha. It's nice to meet you, Dr. Salvatore."

CHAPTER 36

"Are you here to kill me?" He said it with forced nonchalance, but emphasized every other word with the shake of the gun.

Hoffman and Pasha still had their hands up, looks of terror on their faces. I continued staring at the gun as I talked to him, trying to choose my words carefully.

"No, Dr. Salvatore, we are not here to kill you. The truth is, someone has been trying to kill us. And we think it might be the same person, or group of people, that are after you right now." He was thinking about this, I could tell, but was not convinced enough to drop the weapon. "We were friends...I was a friend...of Daniela Portonova."

At this, he let out a heavy sigh, looked at the dirt floor and shook his head. Motioning with the gun toward a small table, he told us to sit down.

"Would anyone like a drink?" he offered politely.

Under these circumstances nobody felt like a glass of wine. Even Hoffman declined.

"Pity," he said. "My collection is rated in the top ten of Italy." He sat down with us, placing the gun on the table. It still held our attention, but at least he had stopped waving it in the general direction of our faces.

Underneath the table lamp, Dr. Salvatore looked less crazed and more like a man who was simply exhausted. I guessed he was in his fifties, a lanky man with deep creases in his face. His eyes drooped, full of spidering red veins. I wondered if he always looked like this, or if he had been hiding out for a while.

He coughed loudly, then said, "Daniela was a beautiful person...so lively and energetic...brilliant...such a loss. How did you know her?"

I recounted the story for him. How we'd met in Chapel Hill. I told him about our strange date, and how she had alluded to the theft of the shroud in hushed tones, but never came out and said what was really going on. That in retrospect she seemed overly suspicious, almost paranoid, that people might be watching her. He nodded gravely. I told him about my interaction with her in the parking lot. And that somehow she slipped a scrap of paper with a series of numbers into my pocket, the address of a website. He couldn't hide a look of surprise and, I thought, admiration, on his face at this point. Slapping the table, he uttered something loudly in Italian, then motioned for me to continue.

Quietly I shared with him how we witnessed her death, from the parking lot below her apartment. He wanted every detail, so I told him as much as I could remember as he stared at me with glassy eyes. The confusion, the police interrogations. Some sleepless nights. I shared with him our discovery of the website and its contents, leaving out the fact that we broke into her office to find the password. With a little computer hacking from Pasha, we discovered who it was behind the user names and, as we studied the information, and put everything together, it seemed clear Daniela's death was just a small part in a much bigger story.

"It seems to be getting much bigger all the time," I commented. He simply nodded again, muttering something to himself.

I shuddered as I recounted the man entering our house and coming after us, and the chase down the road to the airport. Salvatore was amazed we made it to our plane, managing to make it, alive, to London, then Scotland, then here. He had already heard about Larry Beckham's death, but as I told him about the events of earlier today, finding Margie Duncan, he put a hand over his mouth in disbelief, and then hit the table with his fist.

"Bastardos!"

None of us needed a translation for that.

He suddenly put a finger to his lips and motioned for us to be quiet. He jumped up from the table, scurried over to the ladder on the far wall of the wine cellar, and climbed up. Shifting a small brick from the wall, a shaft of light pierced the room, and he squinted, looking through the hole.

"Someone else is here," he whispered. "They are approaching the front door."

He climbed down and made his way to a small desk with a computer.

"My paranoia is finally paying off," he said, as he moved the mouse until he found a screen full of surveillance cameras. Clicking on one positioned right over the front door, we waited. I leaned in as we watched two men make their way up the steps. One was short, heavyset with dark greased-back hair, sunglasses, and a goatee. I did not recognize him. The other man was looking down as he walked up the steps, and seemed to have a limp. There was a bandage around his head but as he looked at the camera, Hoff, Pasha, and I jumped.

"It's him!" Pasha said. He was right. The platinum blonde assassin was back from the dead. And now he had a friend with him. We heard the doorbell chime up above. They waited. We waited, to see what they would do. The assassin motioned to his friend, who leaned down over the door lock out of view.

"He's picking the lock," I said. Less than a minute and they were in.

"Come on, gentlemen," Dr. Salvatore said. "We cannot wait around to see what happens next."

Salvatore grabbed the gun off of the table and walked not up the stairs but instead winding his way through the wine cellar. He was moving fast in the dim light and we were trying to just keep up. We were at the back of the cellar now and I was disoriented. I wasn't sure what part of the house we were under, if we were still under it at all. I noticed another ladder against a wall, and Dr. Salvatore once again climbed.

"Well, don't just stand there and get yourself killed," he leaned back toward us. "Come with me."

At the top, he pushed open a small door in the ceiling and then disappeared. Hoffman was next, then Pasha reluctantly climbed up. I was last and when I emerged through the hole, I realized where we were. Salvatore's garage.

His gleaming, silver Ferrari was beckoning, directly in front of us. Without hesitation, Salvatore pulled the string on the garage door allowing him to operate the metal panel manually. Slowly, as quietly as possible, he raised the door in front of the car. We knew that at any moment the door from the inside to the garage could burst open, and we would be face to face with the assassin again. I kept an eye on the door as Pasha and Hoffman climbed into the back of the car. Salvatore got in, and I jumped into the soft, leather passenger seat.

"Ready?" Salvatore said. When the loud engine started, we might as well have broadcast through a loudspeaker that we were here.

"Ready," I said. He cranked the engine and it purred to life. Speeding out of the driveway, he suddenly brought the car to a stop. Pasha and Hoffman, looking back, saw the door inside the garage swing open.

"What are you doing?" Hoffman said, panicking. "They are coming!"

Salvatore rolled down his window, picked up the gun, and stuck the barrel through the opening.

"Are you going to shoot them?" Pasha said, horrified.

Salvatore didn't respond. He pulled the trigger twice. Two bullets entered two tires of their black sedan. Then he hit the gas and our heads were thrown back into the seats. A spray of bullets hit the gravel behind us and to the side, and a tree just in front of us. A bullet slammed into the car and Salvatore cursed in Italian and pushed the gas harder. Going sixty down a gravel road is not exactly what you want to do in a Ferrari, and we bounced along, our heads hitting the roof. But we made it around a curve, out of the way of their shooting.

"They won't get far with those flat tires," Salvatore exclaimed, a look of glee on his face. In a twisted way, he seemed to be enjoying this. When we hit the pavement, the car launched into another gear and Salvatore skillfully guided us down the one-lane road. I didn't look out my window, to see how close we were to the cliff. The doctor had that wild grin on his face again as he drove.

"Nice car," I said, clutching the armrest.

"Ferrari 612 Scaglietti," he said, beaming. "A present I gave to myself three months ago. Zero to sixty in three point nine seconds. Quite a ride, don't you agree?"

I held on tightly, and I could tell Hoffman and Pasha were doing the same. "Yes, I agree," I said. I wondered if he had some newfound cash as a result of his work on the shroud. I decided it would be bad timing to ask that question in our current situation.

We hit the main road, and I kept looking back, but there was no car chasing us. Salvatore was right. They wouldn't get very far on two bad tires. He was taking no chances, though, and raced us through town.

"I know a safe place," Salvatore said. "We need to talk."

CHAPTER 37

We were in the town of Biella, cruising past people on the narrow streets, vegetable stands, an outdoor market. Salvatore wheeled the Ferrari down a cobblestone alleyway.

"Where exactly are we going?" Hoffman asked.

"And we're going to need to get the rental car back," Pasha chimed in, wedged beside Hoff in the back seat.

He ignored both comments and quickly pulled into an open garage space. Hopping out, he pulled the door down behind us.

"Get out," he said, as he walked up a couple of steps and disappeared through a swinging door. We looked at each other and I shrugged, and followed him through the door.

We were in the back of a restaurant kitchen. Salvatore was speaking in rapid-fire Italian to a man who appeared to be the head chef, standing behind a large flat stove. They were going back and forth and at one point I thought they were arguing, but at the end of the conversation they embraced and kissed each other on the cheek.

Walking out of the kitchen and into the small restaurant, we found a booth in the back, out of sight from the handful of diners. Sitting for the first time in what felt like hours, we realized we were famished. I reminded myself we had been in Scotland that morning, which was hard to believe. It had been a long, long day.

A waitress came up and Salvatore had another long conversation with her and apparently was ordering a lot of food. And most likely, wine. He sent her off, and another waiter came quickly with wine. After Salvatore tasted and approved, he poured for us. She returned quickly with a plate full of antipasti and we dug in.

"Dr. Salvatore," I said, my mouth half-full, "we need to know what is going on. I dragged my friends over here, thinking we were going to find some clues in the death of my friend. I'm a little naïve, perhaps, but I thought we would be able to help the police investigation." I paused. "I'm not very good at sitting around and waiting for somebody to do something."

"I'll drink to that," Hoffman raised his glass and took a big gulp of wine.

"Then things snowballed," I admitted. The understatement of the year. "So we're here, in Biella Italy. In way over our heads." I sipped the wine, rich and red, warm to my stomach.

Salvatore put his glass down on the table. "And yet, you only know one part of the story, gentlemen. There are…how should I say…larger powers at work here. Much larger than you and me. And much more powerful."

More food started arriving. Pasta with different sauces. Meatballs larger than I had ever seen. We continued to fill our plates as we talked.

"We know it revolves around the Shroud of Turin," I said, between bites. "That's why Daniela was killed. And the others."

"Yes," Salvatore said. "You are correct, Matthew."

"I don't understand, though," I said. "The shroud is a relic, an artifact, a historically important find, of course. But it is ancient history. From what I can gather, no one even knows if it is the real thing. I'm sure it is worth a lot of money, but enough to kill someone over? I find that hard to believe."

"Belief," he said, mysteriously, "that is what it is all about, no? Who to believe. What to believe. What you believe about life, about faith, about God, determines so many things, does it not? Whether you have purpose or not. Whether life has meaning or not. Whether there is life beyond what we see. Or not. Belief is a powerful thing. Faith is the strongest element we have in society. It binds people together. It has shaped history."

"It has ruined lives," I suggested.

"Ah, Matthew, this is where you are wrong," he said emphatically. "Belief in God provides us with the ability to see the best in each other and in our world. People have used faith for evil, there is no doubt. But faith in God, in its purest form, is a powerful force in our world for good."

"I still don't understand what this has to do with the shroud," Hoffman said.

Salvatore looked straight at him and leaned forward. "Only everything. Only everything."

He took a long sip of wine and savored it, closing his eyes for a few seconds before he continued.

"The Shroud of Turin has inspired perhaps millions of people in their faith in Jesus Christ as the son of God. Over the centuries, people have viewed it, and many have been strengthened by what it represents. The very burial cloth of Jesus! We have something in our hands that literally enshrouded his body. You cannot get closer to Christ than this."

"Have you seen it before?" I asked. "I mean, actually touched it?"

"Several years ago," Salvatore said, "I was invited for a special, private viewing. You must know, of course, that the Roman Catholic Church keeps it hidden. Once every twenty-five years it is available for a very limited time for the public to view. The rest of the time a replica is on display, at the Church of Saint John the Baptist in Torino. There is no relic they are more adamant about protecting, more paranoid about. Imagine their surprise, then, to find that the real one was stolen." He said this quietly, and my reporter's sense said there was something more there, but I decided not to push it. Yet.

"And so, yes," he said, "I was able to inspect it, to do some testing, to view it up close. It was the highlight of my career. It is what people in my profession dream of doing. Touching something so old. So valuable, and so important. It was magnificent. The image that exists on this cloth. It is hard to explain. Many have come along and presented theories on why the image is there. It is a blood stain, it is a fake from a brilliant artist, and on and on. But what we have found more recently is that it functions much like a photographic negative."

"We know that. But…how?" Hoff said.

Salvatore smiled, picking up his wine glass. "A flash of light, perhaps?" He seemed to be toying with us.

"You're kidding, right?" I said. I was familiar enough with the resurrection story of Jesus, read to my by my mother when I was a kid, then more recently in a religion class in which the professor basically dismantled the core tenets of Christianity—something I secretly enjoyed, watching the "faithful" students squirm in their seats. "You don't really believe that the image was somehow transposed onto the cloth by light, do you? Coming from the body of Jesus?"

"In my field, we work with what we know. When we don't know something, we make the most logical assumptions," he said. "Here is what I know to be true. Every possible explanation we can rule out has been ruled out. The answer to your question is, I don't know. I cannot know. It is impossible for me to draw any firm conclusions with. I can speculate, but who knows? What I do know is that the Shroud of Turin is not a fake. I believe it to be the actual burial cloth that covered the body of Jesus Christ."

"So what was the point of your secret association with these other men and women?"

"Theophilus would have to answer that," he said, now loading his plate with pasta and marinara sauce.

Hoffman, Pasha, and I looked at each other. "We were able to track all of you down. Except Theophilus," Pasha said. "He left no footprints."

Salvatore laughed. "Yes, he is quite elusive. A ghost. He is exceedingly careful. If you find him, it is because he wanted you to. Otherwise, you end up chasing your tail."

I grew frustrated with the conversation. We were talking around in circles and getting nowhere. "So you mean to tell us you don't know why your group was doing all of this extra-curricular work on the shroud?"

Salvatore set his fork down, and sighed, as if trying to decide what he wanted to share. Finally, he said, "I was approached by someone, calling himself Theophilus, to provide my expertise for what he called a 'little project related to the shroud.' He offered to pay me, handsomely, I might add, for my expertise, and so I say to myself 'why not?' I knew others were involved, but at first I only knew them by code name, not face. As for Theophilus, of course I knew this was a code name from the start."

"What does it mean?" I prodded.

"Theophilus?" he raised an eyebrow. "It is from the Bible, the book of Luke and Acts. He supposedly was the audience Luke was writing for, commissioning him to tell the story of Jesus and the early church. It also means lover of God."

"So Theophilus is someone inside the church?" Hoffman asked.

He smiled again. "Hardly. I believe he uses the name in jest."

I brought us back to my main question. "But what did he want to accomplish among the five of you?"

"At first I was in it for the interest, and I am not ashamed to say, for the money." His voice grew lower. "But along the way we discovered something. Something quite extraordinary. Through the work of Margie, Larry, Daniela..." his voice trailed off. Quickly he wiped his napkin across his eyes, tearing up at the mention of the names of his friends. "...and under the watchful eye of Theophilus. A process was discovered, primarily by Duncan, with her unmatched expertise in working with ancient textiles, and then tested and corroborated by the rest of us. The ultimate test has yet to be performed, of course," he said.

I was confused and I could see the same thing on my friends' faces. "What kind of process?"

Salvatore smiled politely, and took another bite of pasta. He wasn't going to tell us. At least, not here. Not now.

"Imagine if a simple piece of cloth that had inspired millions to faith could be used to tear down the very walls of the church it helped build!"

With that, Salvatore excused himself to make a phone call and left us alone in our thoughts.

We ate in silence for a few minutes. I did not know what he meant; how a piece of cloth cause the Church to cave in on itself? What if it really were possible? What was he saying? That somehow the shroud itself was the key to unlocking a truth? A truth the Church would rather not come to light.

I stirred the pasta on my plate, suddenly not so hungry any more.

The reality of what he said was hitting me, and if he was right, it became obvious who was behind the murder of Daniela. And the murders of Larry Beckham and Margie Duncan.

"Time to go," Salvatore said, coming back to the table. "There is someone who would like to meet you."

CHAPTER 38

Cardinal Montenegro stood at the window of his lofty office, staring at the courtyard below. Not many even knew of his existence in the Vatican, let alone the role that he played. There were many spiritual men here, and he intermingled with them when he wanted to, but often was reclusive, holed away in his office or quietly attending to the matters of the Protetterato. Most knew him vaguely by name, and that he was a cardinal of some sort, but no one knew exactly what he did. Well, almost no one. That was how it had to be. How it had been for century upon century for those in his position. For Montenegro and the handful of other resourceful men involved.

He sipped aged brandy as he stood, staring into his glass, and the wrinkled, spotted hand that held it. Many years had he devoted to his position, placing it above family, above friendship. Above everything.

It was another man, comfortable in the shadows, who had recruited Montenegro all those years ago. His mentor, Cardinal Francisco, who was aging and weary after years of the battle.

They were out of the same parish in Rome, Montenegro having risen to prominence under the watchful care of Francisco. Montenegro was from a working-class family on the wrong side of the city, but his mentor had hailed from power, wealth, and position. Although he would never have brought it up in conversation, there was a point where Montenegro was convinced Francisco was in line for the most prominent of positions, the papacy itself.

It never happened, for reasons that didn't become clear until the day Francisco called him into his private offices in the Vatican. Montenegro had never fully understood how his mentor had gained so much good standing, so much power, that he maintained an office here, and the ear of many in the leadership of the Church.

No one else was in his office that day, not a clerk or an assistant. Just Montenegro and Francisco, sitting in red velvet chairs. It was on that day that he learned a secret. One that would alter everything about his life.

Francisco admitted there was a time when he had yearned for the spotlight of the papacy. But he came to realize he was destined for a different path. The details of which even the pope, and other high-ranking officials, were unaware. An aged cardinal had recruited him, many years ago, revealing to him the existence of a secret group of men, protectors. *Il protettores*. Protectors of the church and its interests. And the church, throughout the years, apparently had many interests in need of protection. Not even the pope had access to the history of this group and their dealings within the church, and without. Nothing was written down, no records kept. Montenegro could only imagine what influences this protectorate had exercised upon the world.

He knew now what they were capable of, of course. Affecting world leaders, governments, even installing new leaders when dissatisfaction with an existing regime occurred.

If people only realized.

Taking another sip of brandy, he sat down now in his soft leather chair. Forty years ago, his mentor had asked him for a favor. To become a protector of the Church, of the Cross.

He had no choice in the matter. To decline his prominent friend's request would be to hasten one's exit from any significant role within the Vatican. But to say yes, could lead to many, many opportunities. And it had intrigued him, the secrecy, the power, and the agenda to protect and defend the Church at all costs.

He accepted, and within five years was the head of this secret society that officially did not exist. He learned there were many dangers for the Church to avoid. Many pressures coming, from inside and outside, that needed alleviating. There was much to do.

But leaning his head back now against his chair and closing his tired eyes, he knew nothing the Church had faced over the last forty years had the potential to be as dangerous as this.

And not only dangerous to the Church.

He had a secret of his own that could cause him to come undone.

In front of him on his wide expanse of desk was only one folder. He opened it, thumbing through the latest report assembled by one of his associates.

"Theophilus," he muttered sarcastically. "So it has to come to this."

He'd hoped the situation would be resolved quickly, discreetly, by his men. But so far, at least, they had failed. If this had been years earlier, twenty, or perhaps even ten, what was getting ready to happen would have torn the Cardinal to his core.

He flipped over the summary page to the photographs. Pictures of Daniela Portonova, Larry Beckham, and Margie Duncan, a red stamp over their faces that simply read "eliminated". Followed by snapshots of Matthew Harkin, Hoffman Schwaab, Pasha Griecko, and Andrea Salvatore.

The last picture was not a photo, but a generic silhouette. Underneath it was the name "Theophilus".

Montenegro stared at the image. "Andrew, my brother. I am sorry." He said it without much emotion.

Closing the file, he picked up the phone.

"I've located Theophilus," he said to the waiting voice. "Prepare your men. It's time."

CHAPTER 39

They piled back into the Ferrari and Salvatore quickly pulled out of the alleyway behind the restaurant and back onto this town's sleepy streets. He wasted no time. It would not be difficult for the assassins to see them, if they lingered. Speeding along the narrow road down the mountain, he turned the car to the right on the main highway, toward Turin.

Pasha leaned forward in his seat from the back. "So who is it that would like to meet us?"

Hoffman spoke up. "Good question. We're kind of tired, you see, of getting chased down and shot at." His words clipped along quicker than normal. I couldn't remember seeing him quite this stressed before. "Who is it that wants to meet us? Someone else who is after our butts? I wouldn't mind heading straight for the airport, if you guys want to know the truth."

I couldn't say I disagreed. This journey was bearing down on each one of us. And now we were hurtling down the road in a late model Ferrari with a world-renowned Italian archaeologist. Not exactly the typical road trip.

"I know, guys, I know," I turned around to face them. "I feel the same way. There's a big part of me that just wants to get out of here. I keep pinching myself to see if this is real or not. But we finally found someone who may know what happened to Daniela. Or at least can provide us with some critical information. We finally found somebody alive. That has to count for something, right?" Pasha just stared at me, Hoffman rolled his eyes.

"I have a really good feeling about this," I asserted. "We're getting to the end of the road here. Trust me."

At this they both said nothing, but stared out their windows at the Italian countryside whirring by.

Salvatore cleared his throat. "Theophilus," he said, looking at them in the rearview mirror. "I'm taking you to meet Theophilus. After all you have been through, I figure it's the least I can do. Plus, he told me he wants to meet you."

This captivated even Hoffman's attention.

"Well maybe I don't want to meet him," he said and folded his arms, still staring out the window.

"Ah, but you do not understand," Salvatore said. "It is a rare opportunity you have been given. Not many have seen this man in years. He is a recluse, he remains in his compound and has a handful of servants and bodyguards who are his contact with the outside world. I insist you meet him. Plus, I think you will find he will provide the answers you seek."

"Who is he?" I asked. Salvatore kept his eyes on the road and said nothing.

After thirty minutes, we came upon a curve, with a high craggy mountain on the right, and a dense grouping of bushes on the left. I held onto the armrest, prepared for him to hug the edge of the road and accelerate the explosive engine through the turn, but instead, he turned the car quickly to the left. The unexpected jolt sent Pasha toppling into Hoffman. I thought for sure we were heading into the trees, or worse, off a cliff.

"Where are you—" But before I could finish, a driveway seemed to appear out of nowhere, in-between a set of eucalyptus bushes. "How did you see that?"

The driveway was intentionally hidden from view. I had no idea how Salvatore had seen the entryway. He just smiled, and we began to descend down a hairpin road.

We rounded the next curve and I could finally see where we were headed. Although invisible from the road, a multi-level mansion extended out of the face of the mountain wall. The stone the walls were made of matched the side of the mountain so well that it was hard in some places to tell which was which. I tried to peer down the side of the mountain wall, and I could not see where it stopped. There must have been at least six different levels of house here, all somehow connected.

It impressed even Hoffman, who gave a low whistle. "Sweet place."

We parked in a cobblestone drive that encircled a fountain with an expensive-looking sculpture of a naked woman. A short man whose arms were about to explode out of his grey suit opened the front door before we could knock. He said nothing. I wondered if he was a servant or a bodyguard. Both, I figured, when I saw the gun holster underneath his jacket as he held the door open for us.

Our feet clicked across the marble-floored foyer. The servant-bodyguard ushered us quickly across it, down a set of steps that led to another room with sofas and a piano and the largest glass window I had ever seen. Outside was an unobstructed view of the Mediterranean, all jewel-blue and flat. We didn't stop here, though. Turning a corner to another flight of stairs, we continued to descend into a cozier room, directly underneath, with the same view, but a smaller window. Off to the left was an office, with large glass and mahogany doors that were closed.

"Welcome, gentlemen! Sit down."

The voice crackled behind us, and we turned to meet Theophilus. His cheeks drooped off his face like an old bull dog and he walked along slowly with a carved cane, but his eyes were focused and fiery. A few wisps of white hair clung to the top of his head, as if holding on for dear life.

A man followed him into the room, dressed in a black suit. Eyeing us carefully, he said nothing, and stood off to the side. The imperative to sit apparently did not apply to him.

"Salvatore," he nodded crisply. Andrea Salvatore bowed his head in response.

Theophilus—or whatever his name was—motioned for us to sit. Each of us found a place on two leather sofas, sinking down into the soft cushions. Any other day and it would have been a great location for a nap.

"Anyone want a drink?" he offered. "Carlos makes the best martinis this side of Chapel Hill." He smiled, and Carlos, the servant-bodyguard, nodded. We declined. Theophilus shrugged.

"Scotch, Carlos," he said, slowly sitting down in a chair. He leaned forward on his cane, looking at us, unblinking. "I understand you boys have been on quite a journey." He smiled, though it was the kind that was unreadable. Immediately I got the sense this man would make a great poker player.

"Yes sir, you could say that," I said, looking back at Pasha and Hoffman and then to Theophilus. Pasha sat, leaning forward with his arms resting on his knees, hands sweating as usual. Hoffman had flung himself back on the sofa, head cocked back.

"It started with the death of a...friend of mine, Daniela Portonova." Even now when I spoke her name my stomach jumped.

His face grew dark and in his words I could hear anger and regret. "She was a friend of mine, too. Those responsible for what happened to her will pay for their misdeeds."

I knew he meant it. It set me at ease, believing he might be on our side. I told him our story, just as I had with Andrea Salvatore. He asked a few questions, but mostly sat and listened intently. Much of it he seemed to already know. When I told him about trying to find Beckham and finding out he was dead, and then our visit to Aberdeen and Margie Duncan, anger flashed across his face and he scowled. He stood up as I continued the story, walking over to the window and staring out at the Mediterranean. I told him about finding Salvatore in his house, hiding out from the assassins, and our escape earlier today. He nodded, and for a while the room was silent.

I heard the frustration, the pent-up anger, come out in my own voice, and I could not control it. Nor did I want to. "Can you explain to us, Theophilus, or whatever your name really is, just what is going on?"

He turned to face us again. "How much do you know about the Shroud of Turin?"

More than I ever wanted to, I thought. "It's a historical, religious relic with apparently a lot of significance, more than most people think. What that significance is…" My voice trailed off. That was why we were here. None of us knew.

"What that significance is, Mr. Harkin, is the reason for your visit. It has been my life's work for the last two decades. And now," he said more quietly, "it is the reason that three world-renowned researchers are dead. But their work will not have been done in futility. Not if I have anything to say about it. The ones who killed them, they will soon have much more to deal with than the deaths of three people."

"Who, exactly, killed them?" I said.

"Follow me," he said, ignoring my question and moving down a long hallway to the left. For an old man with a cane, he was quick. We passed room after room, until we came to a library. At the center of the room was a desk, and Theophilus walked over to it and picked up a glass box, holding it up to the light. Inside, there was an ancient scroll.

He pulled a pair of gloves out of a drawer, opened the glass container and placed the scroll on top of the desk, turning on two lamps. Delicately he opened up the scroll and stretched it across the desk. It looked as if it could disintegrate if someone breathed too heavily on it. He placed it down in the center of the desk, beaming at it like a prized possession. We leaned in to have our own look. An ancient writing covered the page out to the edges. The writing was interrupted on the far right side by a diagram of some sort. It looked complex. I was unable to tell what it was at first glance.

"Looks…old," I said, a brilliant observation that Theophilus ignored.

"I found this in 1991, doing excavation work around Jerusalem. I was in an area many scholars thought was a waste of time, but I had reason to believe I would find something significant. We dug for months and found nothing. I financed the venture myself, my own people, my own personal crew, equipment and everything." He waved his hand at some imaginary people. "They thought I was crazy. Foolish, wasteful. But I found something."

He leaned over the page now with satisfaction. "I told myself we had one more week and that was it. And on the second to last day we were there, we uncovered a small hole carved into the base of a rock. So small it could only fit a human hand. I reached in, and put my fingers on this. It was caked with dirt, and as soon as I saw it I knew we had something important."

Pasha spoke up. "So what does it say?"

"It is an instruction manual of sorts," answered Theophilus. "Written by Luke."

"You mean, *the* Luke?" I asked. "From the Bible?"

"Exactly," he beamed.

"Instructions for what?" Hoffman asked.

"How to find the lost tomb of Jesus Christ," he said simply, and walked out of the room.

CHAPTER 40

We followed him back down the hallway to the same room, where he grabbed his drink.

"My name is Andrew Scarlanzi," he said, sipping on his scotch again. "Do you know why I used the name Theophilus?"

"Luke," I said, thinking through what he had just revealed about the document. "Salvatore told us that Luke used the name in his writings in the Scriptures. He was supposedly writing to Theophilus, who had possibly hired him to research and write out the story of Christ and the early church."

"That is correct, Mr. Harkin," he said.

"Hold on a second, Scarlanzi," Hoffman said. "My father dragged me through Jerusalem and the rest of Israel one summer on one of his excursions and we went right to the tomb of Jesus. In fact, I bought a piece of his actual cross around the corner from his tomb. What's the big deal? Everyone knows where it is."

Scarlanzi laughed. "That is not the real tomb, of course. It is a fake, created for tourists like yourself. A place to sell trinkets. A place to link a religious myth with a locale. No one has ever found the real tomb. Not yet, anyway. Some scientists and archaeologists have speculated on it, some have even claimed they have found it. Television programs have even been made," he shook his head. "But none have actually found the authentic resting place of Jesus Christ."

"Then why do they claim that they have?" I asked.

Scarlanzi slumped down in a chair, suddenly looking tired. "The Church claims that location to be the tomb because it has to. It needs to. Millions and millions of people are claiming a belief in something. Imagine if the Church could not produce an empty tomb?"

"What are you saying?"

He shifted in his chair. "When I found the scroll, I knew I had something in my hands that was historic, that was important. I also knew I could not handle it alone. I needed expertise, I needed the smartest people around the table, studying it, researching it, looking at it together. That is how I came to involve these four men and women. I approached them, anonymously at first, offering to pay them for help in a research project related to an ancient manuscript I had discovered, which I believed to be related to the shroud. A few were skeptical at first, but when they realized the document was authentic and I was serious, they each agreed."

"How could we not?" injected Salvatore. "An opportunity to work with an ancient manuscript written by Luke himself? All of us knew this was something special."

"Yes, once you read it, you were very excited," Scarlanzi mused. "Like school kids on the playground. They dove into the work together. All under my watchful eye, of course."

Salvatore grew more and more enthusiastic. "As I worked on the initial translation, I realized what we had. A manuscript that Luke himself had written. Nothing has ever been discovered like this before."

"So this is the actual piece of paper he wrote on?" I asked.

"Not exactly," said Salvatore. "It's a manuscript. A copy of a copy. We believe that this one, though, is one of the earliest examples we've ever found. Dating as early as 200 AD."

"And presumably the other copies..." I said.

"...are either unfound or have been destroyed through the course of time," explained Salvatore.

"In this manuscript," continued Scarlanzi, "we began to discover what amounted to written instructions. Luke was a very meticulous man. You can see that in his biblical writings. He was purported to be a physician, and extremely organized and detailed, leaving nothing to chance. He wrote a manual for how to protect the tomb Jesus Christ was buried in," he said. And then added, "as well as how to find it."

Pasha, who had been mulling this over, spoke up. "Why would they have to protect it, or find it? Wouldn't it have been common knowledge where this tomb was if Jesus really rose from the dead, as they claimed?"

"It is a good question, and there are speculations on the answer," he replied. "What we know is this. The tomb was either hidden or lost. The Roman authorities wanted it destroyed. They wanted it to disappear. Christianity was the scourge of society and a bane to their existence and initially they fought it fiercely. They would have tried to destroy any evidence of the tomb. They wanted to wipe Christians and their upstart religion off the face of the earth. Anyone caught talking about an 'empty tomb' or the 'risen Savior,' was imprisoned or, worse, they suffered the same death as their leader, Jesus."

"So Luke devised a system," Salvatore continued. "An order, a secret society—protectors—an inner group of disciples who would dedicate themselves to guarding the identity of the tomb. They believed God would at some point direct them to reveal the location of the tomb to the world but, until that time, these men were sworn to protect its location with their lives. So a secret society was developed. Il Prottetorato. The Protectors. A group of men trained to guard the secret of the tomb of Jesus with their lives. Passed on from generation to generation, a clandestine group kept secret even from the pope."

"The interesting thing is," he said, sitting forward in his chair, "Luke speaks several time in the manuscript of a key."

"What kind of key?" I said. "Like, to unlock the door of the tomb?"

"No," he said. "A key to help us find it."

"It was Daniela who finally cracked the code in the manuscript," added Salvatore. "There is a diagram

169

contained in the document. It was so cryptic, with no wording, simply a drawing, that all of us were stumped. It was Daniela who discovered the key."

It finally clicked with me. "The Shroud of Turin."

"Yes," Scarlanzi said, slapping his hand down on the chair. "Luke is telling us the shroud itself is the key to finding the lost tomb of Jesus Christ."

CHAPTER 41

"From the earliest days of the church, the shroud was revered," Scarlanzi said. "It was hidden away, thought to possess miraculous powers, even healing qualities. It was lost for a while but found again by a knight in the middle ages. The shroud was returned to this group of protectors, who knew very well the secrets that it kept, bound by Luke himself to keep it safe at all costs."

Salvatore chimed in. "We still don't understand everything about this amazing cloth. Even Professor Duncan, who examined it thoroughly, has been perplexed. It is mysterious. As I told you already, no one knows what the image is made of, why it is there, or how the impression was created."

"But we think the good doctor Luke knew its secrets," said Scarlanzi. "It is medically accurate in its entirety, including scars on the hands and feet of the body. Regardless of how it was created, we now believe we know what it was created to do. Daniela realized the diagram was actually a map. Of the location of the tomb. And the shroud is the key to finding it. The diagram is a picture of the shroud positioned precisely, at a location in Jerusalem. When the sun shines at a very particular angle, somehow the shroud illuminates the location of the tomb."

"The Shroud of Turin is actually some kind of lens that the sun shines through?" Pasha said.

"Precisely," Salvatore said, gleaming.

"So you stole it and somebody wants it back," I said, standing up. "Are you telling me a group of priests killed these people? They sent a hit man to kill Daniela? Do you realize how ridiculous that sounds?"

My head was reeling. This was too much to wrap my mind around, too much to believe.

"I do not believe it is far-fetched," Scarlanzi said quietly. "In fact, I know this to be fact. But they didn't do it just because they want their property back. It's because they are afraid."

"Of what?" Hoffman asked.

"The truth," he muttered. "That if we find the real tomb of Jesus, we'll expose the Church for a fraud. That inside we will find the bones of Jesus himself."

I did the math. "No Jesus risen from the grave, no empty tomb, equals no religion."

"And therefore, no church," added Salvatore.

"And we know they can't afford that," Scarlanzi said. "Especially not the inside few. The Church is a well-oiled machine, a business. And a highly profitable one too, I might add. Imagine if it came to light that Jesus never really rose from the grave? That he was buried, like any other man. Jesus, just an ordinary guy."

"Do you think there are people in the church who really believe that?" I asked.

"Il Protterato does," Scarlanzi said. "The protectorate still exists. Morphed over centuries into some kind of over-resourced, hyper-powerful group of men, clinging to their positions of authority and living in hypocrisy. I should know. Their leader came to me on behalf of their rogue group repeatedly when somehow he learned of my discovery of the Lukan writing. They wanted to buy it from me. Over and over he came, and each time I refused. Finally he had his goons threaten me, but nothing came of it. They are deeply afraid of this discovery, that much is clear. And why shouldn't they be? They are profiting from an organization based upon a lie!" He pounded his cane as he said these words. "None of them believe what they claim to believe any more. They are as sure as I am that when we open the tomb we will find the bones of Jesus, there for all the world to see. And then what will become of their mighty Church?"

The words echoed loudly in the room where we sat. Again, he slumped back into his chair and spoke quietly.

"I had my men orchestrate a theft," he said. "The Shroud of Turin was borrowed from the Church of Saint John the Baptist. It was a quite beautiful operation." He held his glass up to the silent man standing against the wall, who nodded appreciatively.

"Il Protetterato began tracking us down. They found out about our research project," he said. "They located all of us. And one by one they have stalked and murdered us. There were five. Now there are only two left. And because, well, you three just can't seem to let it go, they are coming after you as well."

Hoffman and Pasha were turning various shades of pale.

"We've got to get out of here," Hoff said, his voice quavering. I could see he was finally breaking down. "I just want to go home, to get back to my life, and pretend like this never happened."

"You can't," Scarlanzi countered. "You have witnessed too much now, way too much. You cannot go back to your life, pretending like nothing ever happened. They won't allow it. I won't allow it."

"How can you stop me?" Hoffman said, standing. "I can walk out of here right now, get back on a plane and head home. In fact," he said, heading toward the door, "that's what I'm going to do. I'm out of here."

"If you go now," Scarlanzi called to him, "I would wager you will not make it to the airport alive. You do not understand the full scope and power of this group of men. They have people everywhere and resources at their disposal. They obviously know you are here. How would they not know if you got back on a plane?"

His words stopped Hoffman in his tracks. He breathed a heavy sigh and turned back around. "You're saying we're stuck here?"

"I am saying," Scarlanzi emphasized, "you are in the safest place possible right now. And I can ensure you are delivered properly back to your homes. After this is over."

"What does that mean, exactly, after this is over?" asked Pasha.

"After they have been exposed, after the Church has been exposed, as frauds, of course," Scarlanzi said plainly.

"What, do you plan to keep us hostage or something?"

He smiled. "Of course not, Matthew. I plan to ask for your help. But I have one more thing to show you."

CHAPTER 42

We entered his office and Scarlanzi reached up on his bookshelf, pushing a button. A single elevator door opened in the wall.

"Cool," Hoff admitted, reluctantly still with us.

We climbed aboard, Scarlanzi swiped a card through a slot, and we began descending to B2. Two levels below ground.

"You will be the first people outside our five to see this room," he said.

We exited the elevator and entered a room that was dark, except for the center, which glowed with an other-worldly light.

Extended fully on a table in front of us was the Shroud of Turin.

"So, you do have it," I said, walking to the edge of the table. Hoffman, Pasha, and I approached it slowly, in reverence for the mysterious artifact. It had not only impacted untold numbers for centuries, it had turned our own lives upside down.

It must have been fourteen feet long and about four feet across. It was worn in places but remarkably intact. The image was blurry at first, but as I looked closer at the brownish colorings on the cloth, I started to make out a head, a body. And then arms and the feet. Looking even closer, I saw what might be holes in the feet and hands, and markings along the man's head. Allegedly, wounds from a crown of thorns. I moved toward the face, which was remarkably detailed. It was a ghostly image and I quickly found myself transfixed by it. Could it really be what they said it was?

"It is amazing, is it not?" Salvatore said quietly. "I have handled it many times now, but each time I see it, it is like something new again."

Pasha and Hoffman moved close. Hoffman reached out a hand toward the ancient fabric.

"Please!" Salvatore said, grabbing his arm. "Do not touch. It exists here under special lighting that does not affect the fabric. But human touch disintegrates it rapidly. The oils in the skin and such."

We were mesmerized by this centuries old relic. *The cloth that touched Jesus himself*, I kept thinking. I was not a religious person. But my mother had instilled within me a sense of spirituality. Something about being in the presence of the shroud stirred something deep inside.

Something else welled up, though. Anger. I thought about Daniela, and how this piece of cloth had led to her murder. And the others. How could God let this happen? What was the point? I felt my face begin to fluster with rage and I turned away.

"Are you alright, Mr. Harkin?" Scarlanzi asked, eyeing me warily.

I ignored the question, snapping, "What's the plan?"

He raised an eyebrow, and opened his mouth to speak, but I cut him off.

"What are we going to do?" I demanded. "Because I can't just—"

A voice interrupted me, crackling across the intercom system by the elevator door. It was Scarlanzi's man from upstairs, calling for him.

"Sir! We have company! Four men just drove up and broke the door down and—"

The sound of gunfire hissed through the static of the speaker. We heard a scream, then a quiet moan. Then nothing.

The clap of footsteps rang through the same speaker, louder and louder. Suddenly another voice came across the system.

"Andrew? Are you still there? Pick up. Your dear old brother wants to have a chat."

Scarlanzi's face fell ashen. He placed his hand behind him on the wall to try to maintain his balance, and half-fell, half-slid down the wall to the floor, the receiver still in his hand.

"Your brother?" I said. "Your brother is part of The Protectorate?"

Scarlanzi nodded, his eyes closed. "He is its head. He has been for many years."

He lifted the receiver to his mouth. "So, Angelo, it comes to this?"

A calm, assured voice came through the speaker. *"You knew that it would. I tried to stop it from happening. This you must know. I did everything within my power."*

Scarlanzi scoffed. "Everything within your power? Then why are you standing in my house? Killing my men? Have you even stopped to think about what it is you are doing? Who it is you are a part of?"

"There you go again, brother. You have not changed. Lecturing, chastising. Yet you yourself haven't stopped to consider that it is you, in fact, who are on the wrong side. The Church stands against you."

"The Church stands . . . " he mumbled. "You are not the Church!"

Angelo chuckled again. *"You're idealism is admirable, as it always was. But pointless. You had your opportunity to cooperate. We are coming for the shroud, and we are coming for you. Soon, you will all be dead."*

Static came across the speaker. Then the elevator began to move. It was moving downward. Scarlanzi awoke from his daze and sprung up from the ground.

"The shroud!" he said. "Get it!"

Now was not the time to be careful. Salvatore grimaced, touching it as delicately as possible, but quickly folded it up.

Scarlanzi pointed to a door. "In the closet, there's a black duffel."

Pasha opened the closet door and grabbed the bag, tossing it to Salvatore. He threw in the shroud put the bag on his back.

"Is there an exit down here?" I asked. "Stairs? A way out besides the elevator?"

Scarlanzi nodded, pushing off on his cane toward a door in the corner. "This way, gentlemen. Two flights of stairs to ground level, then there's an exit outside. If we can get to the garage and a car, perhaps we can escape."

The stairwell looked like it went six or seven flights up. We went down two levels, and headed out a door that opened up onto a narrow walkway. To the left was a rock trail that looked like a maintenance path. It was just wide enough for a work cart to drive back and forth. At the edge of the trail was a cliff that must have dropped down one hundred feet or so, rocks and water below. To the right was another small set of stairs, leading straight up a hill with a gate at the top.

"At the top of the steps," Scarlanzi said, "it opens up into the driveway. If we hurry, we can make it up there and be gone."

"Salvatore," I said," give me the bag." I held out my hand to him.

He hesitated. "What, are you crazy?"

"Take the shroud out, and give me the bag," I said again, with a calm that surprised even me. It hit me that this is what dad probably would have done. "Pasha, Hoffman, get these guys up the steps and to safety."

They began to protest. I put my hand up. "We don't have time to argue. Salvatore, give me the bag, stuff the shroud in your shirt. Do it, now!"

Reluctantly, he did as I instructed. I put the bag on my back.

"Don't worry," I nodded, even smiling. "I'll meet you at the airport."

There was no time for good-byes. "One more thing, Salvatore," I said, holding up my hand. "The keys to the Ferrari."

Eyeing me suspiciously, he took them out and tossed them in the air. I caught them and took off down the path.

I heard them scramble up the steps behind me. Positioning myself around the corner from the door, I made sure I was close enough for the goons to see me.

After all, that's what I wanted.

I didn't have to wait long. The door burst open and I saw a gun emerge, followed by a man with sunglasses and a dark suit. He turned toward me just as I let the stone I had been holding in my right arm fly. Three years of little league pitching paid off in less than a second. The rock crashed across his forehead and sent him to the ground. A crushing eighty-mile per hour fastball. I saw blood spurt, but I didn't wait for him to get up. I heard him screaming as I took off down the trail.

"That way!" I heard someone say. "He has the shroud!"

I was running, hard, uphill on the trail. Slipping on a loose rock, I glanced back long enough to see two men turn the corner. One was the blond, thin man, with sunglasses on, and a bandage across his face. My old friend had survived the bookshelf falling on him after all. A new burst of energy led me further up the trail, and I felt a bullet graze past my head just before a tree branch exploded in front of me. The trail curled around into the brush and, temporarily at least, it hid me from their sight.

Gunfire again, this time wildly spraying into the woods. I dropped, landing stomach to the ground as bullets whizzed over me. Once they seemed to be moving again, and not shooting, I hopped up. The trail forked in front of me. To the left, it seemed to move back toward the house. The right path continued along the side of the cliff. I could head back to the house. But it also would lead them back toward everyone else, and it was possible my friends hadn't had a chance to get to the car yet. I didn't want to take that risk.

I scurried to the right, assuming they would split up. At least I would only have to deal with one of them. If I could just waste enough time, then I could figure out how to get out of here somehow.

Just then, two bullets screamed past me, breaking off a chunk of rock and sending it down the cliff side.

"Harkin!"

I stopped. They were close. Suddenly, there was nowhere to go.

Raising my hands, I turned, and saw the blonde man pointing his gun at me.

"This is the third time this week you've done that," I said, forcing my hands to stop shaking.

His lips curled up slightly, aimed the gun squarely at my head, and squeezed the trigger.

I closed my eyes and waited for the inevitable. I wondered if the bullet hitting my skull would lead to unimaginable pain or feel like nothing at all.

Click.

He was empty. My eyes were in an instant drawn behind him, to the craggy cliff and the drop below.

Suddenly all the anger, the frustration, the rage I felt from Daniela's murder, to the dead professors, to being chased and shot at, to my father's death, exploded within me. I ran straight at him, letting out a primal sound from deep within as I charged. He tried to swing the gun at me like a hammer but I felt the gun glance across my cheek. I caught him square in the sternum. At contact, I heard the crack of ribs in his chest. I was low and leaned up into his body and, in an instant, he was up off of his feet. The force of my blow pushed him to the edge of the cliff and then, as I dropped to the ground, he fell backwards, off the trail. Off the cliff.

Down, down, down.

I caught my breath and looked over, to the craggy waters below. His body lay awkwardly on a rock, unmoving.

"Oh, God," I whispered. I suddenly felt like throwing up.

CHAPTER 43

I ran back toward the house hunched low, unsure of where the other man had gone, or even how many there really were. I assumed the blonde man's associate had gone down the path back toward the house. I stayed along the edge of the woods, crouching. It made for slower going, but it seemed safer. I soon saw the house, windows glinting through the trees.

My eyes caught movement on the front porch and I quickly ducked behind a tree. Peering around, I saw an old man, smoking a cigarette and pacing. He held his head high with a scowl on his face. This was Scarlanzi's brother. I was sure he was waiting for his men to report in.

He finally flicked the cigarette butt off the porch and walked back into the house. It was the only chance I needed. I was in a full sprint toward the Ferrari when out of the corner of my eye I noticed a long, black Mercedes that had been recklessly pulled to a stop to the left of the house, nose facing the cliff. The cliff overlooking the crystal clear waters of the Mediterranean.

It would be a clear shot.

I slid low around to the driver's side door and tested it. It opened. The high-pitched buzz told me the keys were in the ignition.

"Alright then," I whispered to myself, glad to finally have something go my way. I stuck my foot inside the car and touched the brake, and then reached across to the gearshift, tugging it into neutral. The car was already on a slight decline, and a small push sent the front tires creeping off the brick driveway and onto the sandy surface. I wish I could have watched it roll, but I had been in the driveway too long already. I ran over to the Ferrari and held the door open long enough to hear the sickeningly delightful sound of crashing metal and glass in the distance, two hundred feet below.

The Ferrari's engine roared through my feet. I felt it up my legs and into my spine. It was exhilarating. Slamming the gas pedal down, the car nimbly responded and I exploded up the driveway. I curled around the long drive, hit the main road, made that engine roar again, and I was gone.

CHAPTER 44

I was staring out the plane window when I caught my first look at the Middle Eastern desert. It stretched out in all directions, an expanse of yellow and brown that brought to my stomach a growing pit of nerves. We were close.

It hadn't taken me long to catch up with the others. The call from Hoffman had come through on my cell not long after I had sped away from Scarlanzi's house. Soon we were packed in a plain white bus, like tourists heading back to the airport. At least we didn't have to fly commercial this time. Scarlanzi had a private jet, and I flung myself down into a soft leather passenger chair.

I wanted to go home. I was tired. My friends were worn thin, beaten down by the chase of the last few days. Emotionally, we were tattered. I felt on edge, and I found myself snapping at Pasha, at Hoffman, and at the two flight attendants. And yet there was still a pull, a tug. I wanted to know the truth. I wondered if my father felt this same passion well up inside him when he knew he was close to a big break in a story. I knew we were close. I could feel it. If Scarlanzi was right, we would be witness to one of the greatest discoveries in human history.

Salvatore had given Pasha a video camera, which he was now turning over in his hand. It was now his job to capture everything on film. He fiddled with it in his seat and passed the time reading the instruction manual.

I glanced over at Hoffman. His mouth was hanging open and he snored. His head kept leaning over onto Salvatore, seated beside him, who pushed it back each time, glaring. I couldn't blame Hoff. If I could have slept I would have. My body told me I needed to rest but my mind would not stop churning.

Salvatore moved over to sit beside me, clutching the duffel at his side. Even on the private plane, he wouldn't let go of it.

I eyed him. "I wanted to ask this back at the house, but obviously we ran out of time. I still don't get it. Where do we go when we get there? To Jerusalem? How is the shroud supposed to tell us where this tomb is?"

Salvatore's eyes twinkled again as he reached into his bag. He removed the ancient scroll.

"Luke's making the journey with us?" I observed. He nodded, placing the scroll on the table in front of us.

He unrolled it all the way, dust lifting off of the ancient page.

"This is what we have studied for so long," he said, his fingers hovering just over the letters. He then pointed to a drawing at the bottom. "Especially this."

I leaned forward to study the markings. I wasn't sure what to make of it. "All I see here are a handful of lines, pointing in different directions, and a rectangle. Then some words below." I bit my lip, then looked back at Salvatore. "What am I missing here?"

"To the untrained eye, there is nothing here," he said. "In fact, it took us a significant amount of time to understand this. It was only until recently that we knew what it meant, and that was thanks to Daniela. As I've said, she's the one who cracked the code." He pointed to the words, just above the drawing. "The lines and the rectangle you see are impossible to understand without this."

I strained my eyes at the words above. "It's still Greek to me, doctor. What is it?"

"The Phos Hilaron," he said, grinning. I blinked at him, and he waved his hand in the air, dismissive. "Of course you wouldn't know what that is, either. It's the oldest of hymns in the Christian church. Until this document, the earliest written copy we had of the song was from the late third century. But here it is, in this document, which is much older. Now we know Luke himself was the author. Or at the very least, he was aware of the song during his time."

"So maybe he wrote a hymn," I said. "A lot of the early fathers of the church did that, didn't they?"

"Yes, they did," he mused. "And taken by itself, it would not have much significance. But paired with the drawing, you can begin to see what he was up to."

He pushed his reading glasses onto his nose, glancing down at the ancient script, and began to translate.

*"O Light gladsome of the holy glory of the Immortal Father
the Heavenly, the Holy, the Blessed, O Jesus Christ
having come upon the setting of the sun, having seen the light of the evening
we praise the Father, the Son, and the Holy Spirit: God
Worthy it is at all times to praise Thee in joyful voices
O Son of God, Giver of Life, for which the world glorifies Thee."*

He removed his glasses and placed them on the table.

"Alright," I said slowly. "It's a nice hymn. I'm missing the connection to Luke's doodling here."

"You are a reporter, are you not?" He sighed, losing his patience. "There are two things of note here. One is in the text, and another is not. Luke is not only recording an ancient hymn, he is leaving us a clue. Found in the third line."

I thought about the words he'd spoken. "The setting of the sun? The evening light?"

He nodded rapidly. "Yes, yes! And what does it say it does, this evening light?"

It took me another minute. "I think it said it leads us to the worship of Jesus Christ, but…"

"That's right!" he said, slapping his hand on the table. "It says that the light of the setting sun leads us to the Christ himself."

"But that seems like just a metaphor," I said. "A figure of speech. It's what writers do. The hymn writer is just painting a picture of what it looks like to…be religious, or whatever."

185

"In and of itself, yes," he said, sitting back in his seat. "He is simply writing a song for the faithful to sing. But that doesn't take into account the second thing to know. The Phos Hilaron is rumored to have originated in a specific church in Jerusalem. An ancient church, one of the first. It's called the Church of the Holy Sepulchre. Someone in this church wrote this hymn."

Salvatore pointed back to the drawing. "This rectangle here is the shroud. These lines here, Daniela surmised that they represent light."

I held my finger over the line, moving it along. "So this light comes from the shroud, pointing downward."

"Not from the shroud," he said. "But perhaps through it."

"Through it…" My mind wandered back to my conversation with Daniela that night. How some believed the shroud acted like a film negative. It began to make sense. I studied the drawing again. "If the light is going through, where is it coming from? And where does it go? The lines don't seem to lead to anything."

He sat back slowly, rubbing his eyes. "They will, Matthew. They will. We will all see where they lead soon enough."

CHAPTER 45

Our flight touched down in Jerusalem and we quickly exited the plane and loaded into a suburban waiting for us just off the runway. I had never seen anyone Scarlanzi's age move so quickly. He was seized by the adventure in front of us, and was even playfully joking with Pasha and Hoffman.

"You know where to take us," he said to Salvatore as he climbed into the passenger seat.

Salvatore nodded, putting the car into gear. "The Church of the Holy Sepulchre."

Scarlanzi looked at his watch, then up into the sky. It was already late afternoon, and not a cloud in the sky. "I think our timing will prove to be good."

I sat in the back, beside Hoffman and Pasha, who had begun filming already. While his enthusiasm seemed to be growing, Hoffman was still shaking his head, trying to fully wake up from his nap on the plane, and in a foul mood.

"We're almost to the end, Hoff," I said. "Just hang in there a little longer."

"I believe you've said that a few times on this trip," he grumbled, folding his arms and gazing through the opposite window. "This is it for me, okay? The last place I'm going. Next stop from here is North Carolina. No more of this. Do you realize how many calls I've ignored from my dad?" He held up his cell phone before tossing it onto the seat.

I tapped my fingers against the window and studied the ancient city, whizzing by as Salvatore made a series of lefts and rights. "I totally agree."

We zipped through the city streets for twenty minutes, until we finally entered a crowded alleyway. Salvatore parked behind a row of vehicles, and we climbed out, standing on the dusty stone road.

People were milling around the large stone building in front of us, crowds moving in and out of the front doorway. Scarlanzi made sure Pasha had the camera trained on him as he stood in front of it.

"Here we are, finally," his voice quivered, eyes widened with the excitement of a six-year old. "The Church of the Holy Sepulchre. This is the place that, after all our research, after years of careful study, and after several people lost their lives, this is where we have been led."

He turned toward the church, seemingly oblivious to the dozens of tourists surrounding him.

"This place looks old," said Hoffman.

I eyed him. "Doesn't get any older than this, Hoff. For a church."

Pasha held the camera down at his side. "Does he expect us to just walk in and do some kind of experiment in front of all these people?"

A step ahead of us, I could see Salvatore smile. "You should know by now Mr. Scarlanzi never goes anywhere without a plan."

Scarlanzi reached the door ahead of us and spoke to a security guard who was leaning back against a column. The guard seemed disinterested until Scarlanzi withdrew an envelope from his pocket.

"He's bribing him," Hoffman muttered. "Which kind of impresses me."

"On the contrary," answered Salvatore. "He's explaining to this man that we are from a research institute dedicated to the study of ancient artifacts and structures from Europe. We are simply reserving the building to conduct our experiments." He winked at us.

Scarlanzi passed the envelope to the guard, who peeked at its contents and suddenly shouted orders to his colleagues inside. They quickly ushered the other visitors out of the church while setting up a series of stanchions to keep them out.

As we walked inside the guard nodded to us and slammed the door shut. Without the sunlight pouring in through the doorway, the atrium was lit only by lamps, candles, and dim light coming through the windows, casting a golden glow.

"Wow," I said, looking up at the ornate ceiling. But Scarlanzi and Salvatore wasted no time admiring the walls, the ceilings, or the various altars.

They were looking at the windows.

Two windows soared upward in front of us, grand and tall, rising from floor to ceiling.

Scarlanzi quickly shuffled past them. "That's not what we're looking for," he said. He walked through an arched doorway. We followed him into a smaller area with a lower ceiling, though much more ornate. There was gold everywhere, and an altar against the far wall, lit by hanging lamps. The ceiling was detailed with an enormous painting of angels and other characters from the Bible, I assumed. There were two smaller windows, made with intricate stained glass on either side.

He barely stopped to look at them. He was pushing forward, deeper into the old church.

"Does the old guy know where he's going?" Hoffman asked, trailing in the rear. No one responded, probably because it seemed obvious he was indeed looking for something specific.

We continued on, through several small chambers, until we entered a room and Scarlanzi stopped in his tracks. An ancient mural was painted on the floor, roped off so visitors wouldn't be able to walk across it. One solitary window cast its light across the floor. It had to be facing west, because light from the setting sun was pouring inside, ever so slowly creeping along the mural. The painting was unusually tall.

"What is the picture on the floor?" Pasha asked as he held the camera in his hands, filming the scene at his feet. It was a faded pastoral image, sheep grazing, hills behind them, with a painted sun half-visible, blazing across the countryside. A group of shepherds sat in the distance. The image was on one large piece of flat stone.

"It's said this is one of the few remaining original artifacts from the first church structure," Salvatore said, kneeling down to study it. "The church was torn down early on, and eventually rebuilt. Somehow, this piece was protected and it remained. It may be the oldest artifact here."

Scarlanzi was ignoring the painting, however. He was looking closely at the window. "This is it," he muttered to himself. "This is the one."

He turned to Salvatore and nodded. Salvatore slid the backpack off of his shoulder and unzipped it. He carefully removed the Shroud of Turin.

CHAPTER 46

Salvatore handed the ancient relic to Scarlanzi and then disappeared around a corner.

"Where are you going?" Hoffman called out, but he didn't answer.

Salvatore held the cloth with both hands, continuing to stare up at the window, measuring the amount of sunlight pouring through. "We don't have much longer," he said, checking his watch. "Salvatore! Hurry up!"

His cry echoed through the chambers around them. After another minute, something rattled, like metal banging on a wall. All of us flinched. But it was Salvatore, reappearing, this time carrying an extension ladder.

"I figured they had to have some modern day technology stashed around here," he said, holding up the ladder. "For cleaning lamps and windows, I imagine."

He quickly set it up alongside the tall window. Scarlanzi handed him the shroud. Carefully unfolding it, Scarlanzi held the bottom of it while Salvatore held the top corner, walking up the ladder.

When he drew even with the top of the window, he motioned down to me. "Look in the bag, and give me the roll of tape."

I reached into the bag and found the grey roll, holding it up. "Are you telling me you're getting ready to duct tape the Shroud of Turin?"

He snapped his fingers. "Just toss it up here."

"Okay," I said, throwing it up to him. "I didn't think scientists would do something like that, but whatever."

"There's no other way right now," he muttered, pulling the tape out with his teeth and tearing off a large piece.

As carefully as he could, he attached the tape to the shroud and stuck it to the top of the window, so the cloth matched up with the window. Scarlanzi used the taped to secure the bottom section.

"It's the same size as the window," Pasha said, as he panned the video camera up and down. "Exactly."

Once the other side was attached, we could see this was indeed true. The shroud matched up perfectly with the window.

But that realization was quickly overshadowed by what began to happen through the shroud itself. The light from the setting sun shone through it and, as it did, the glow inside the room changed. The bright light became darker, almost red.

It was hard to tear my eyes away from the window, but the image on the floor drew my attention. The floor painting of the countryside scene had darkened as well, almost as if a cloud were hovering over it.

Except for one single point of light. It shone on the grassy pasture among the shepherds and sheep, but was moving. I turned to see the point of light coming from the faded image of the head on the shroud. Near the top, as if it were an illuminated jewel in a crown.

"Look at this!" Scarlanzi said, pointing to the light on the floor. "It's moving, in accordance with the setting sun."

Salvatore was just as excited. "Are you getting all of this, Pasha? Make sure you are recording it!"

Pasha nodded, giving him the thumbs up, the camera to his eye.

The light was moving quickly, across the grassy fields as the sun set. It came to the hills. Suddenly, a glistening jewel exploded with light.

"What's that?" I asked. "I didn't notice it before."

"A hidden jewel in the artwork," Salvatore said. "It seems that somehow it's only visible when this light hits it."

As soon as we saw it, it was gone, as the beam from the shroud continued moving along the picture.

"Could that be it?" Scarlanzi asked as he pointed to the spot on the floor. So quietly it was almost to himself. "Could this be where the tomb of Christ exists?"

I grabbed the duct tape from Salvatore and tore off a small piece. Leaning into the middle of the picture on the floor, I marked where the bright spot had been.

"At least now we'll remember where it was," I said. I figured if they could stick tape to the Shroud of Turin, they wouldn't mind if I did the same to the floor.

We fell into silence as we studied the mark in the middle of the scene. The light from the shroud drifted across the floor, off of the image, and onto the wall. A minute more and it was gone. The shroud looked like the shroud again.

Hoffman asked the obvious question. "Does anyone know where this is?"

Salvatore cleared his throat. "There don't appear to be any obvious markings..."

"...telling us where this is," Scarlanzi said, finishing his sentence.

I reached into my pocket, grabbed my phone, and snapped a picture of the image. I eyed Salvatore.

"Did you see access to the roof anywhere in here?"

CHAPTER 47

We found an old ladder that led through the ceiling of an adjacent room and carefully made our way up. Above it, another ladder shot upward, heading to a square trap door.

I scrambled up and pushed it open. Dust fell around me. I brushed it out of my eyes and pulled myself into a bell tower. The others squeezed themselves into the space, just big enough for the five of us.

The sun cast its fading light on the top of the church, as well as the vast array of buildings across the city laid out below us, and then onto the green land in the distance.

"How exactly are we supposed to know where to go from here?" Hoffman asked.

I held my phone in my hands, the picture of the floor displayed. Like everyone else, I scanned the horizon.

Scarlanzi impatiently grabbed my phone from my hands. "There are three hills in the distance in the floor image. The jewel indicating the location of the tomb is directly in the center of those hills. Now if we can just find…"

"Right there," Pasha said, pointing in the distance.

Three mounds rose up in the distance, above the buildings below. I checked other directions, to be sure.

"He's right," I said. "There aren't any other hills or mountains in sight."

Salvatore grabbed the phone. "Let me see that," he said, studying the picture carefully. He glanced back and forth at the hills and the picture. "If the placement of the jewel on the floor is correct, then it appears as though the tomb would be located near the top floor of that building pushing into the center hill."

There was a large white building backed up to the small mountain.

"Looks like some kind of apartment building, maybe?" I said.

"Let's go," said Scarlanzi, already stepping down onto the ladder. "We know where to look now, at long last."

Salvatore went down, then Pasha and Hoffman behind. I hit the floor of the church last. Everyone was standing still.

"Guys," I said, turning around, "don't we need to get…"

I realized why they were frozen in place.

"Looks like we've caught up with you just in time."

The voice filled up the chamber. I turned to see a gray-haired man standing with a guard on either side, their guns trained on us.

"Andrew," Cardinal Montenegro said, wryly smiling, eyeing Scarlanzi. "I didn't want it to have to come to this."

Scarlanzi stepped forward, pointing his finger at his brother's chest, his eyes widening. "When will you stop, Angelo? When will your quest to cover up the truth end? You—"

He lunged forward wildly with both hands outstretched, reaching for his brother's neck. Montenegro remained still, smirking, as both of the guards stepped in front of him. One of them raised the butt of his weapon and crashed it into Scarlanzi's forehead. He crumpled to the ground, letting out a strange growl as he fell.

Montenegro beckoned to me.

"Your phone."

One of the guards took a step toward me, motioning with his gun for me to hand my phone over.

"Fine, Cardinal," I said, tossing it to him. He caught it and grinned, studying the image. He looked down at the image on the floor, then back at my phone. He nodded toward the ladder. "I'm assuming, based on this picture and your view from the roof, you know where the tomb of Christ is. Am I correct?"

"Yeah, that's right," Hoffman said, before I could stop him. I grabbed his arm and squeezed it, hard, managing a small smile.

"We don't really know what we're looking at," I offered, trying to downplay it. "It's just a dot of light on the floor. It could be anything."

"I don't think so," Montenegro said, staring at my phone again. He pointed to Hoffman. "I think this young man is correct. You know, don't you? You know where it is."

I didn't know what else to say, but I knew this wasn't good. I watched Scarlanzi move slowly, still curled up on the cold floor.

The cardinal clasped his hands together. "The good news, at least for me," he said, clearing his throat, "is everyone who knows about the real tomb is either in this room, or already dead."

CHAPTER 48

Montenegro tossed my phone up and down in his hand and, then, without warning, threw it down onto the stone floor. The screen shattered. He ground the remains under his heel until the power died and it was in a dozen pieces.

"I'm not sure my phone insurance is going to cover that," I said, staring at the glass and metal at his feet.

They escorted the five of us outside, threatening that any move to run would be met with lethal force. After witnessing how Montenegro treated his own brother, I didn't doubt them. We walked slowly back down the Jerusalem street, to our van. I imagined we must have been a strange sight but no one seemed to pay us much attention.

The guards opened the van doors and ushered us inside. Hoffman was moving slowly, on purpose, but they pushed him forward.

"Alright, alright!" he said, raising his hand up and climbing in.

One of the guards sat in the driver's seat, while Montenegro found the front seat beside him. The other guard sat beside us, his gun raised.

Pasha whispered. "They're going to kill us, Matthew! What else would we be doing here?"

My mind raced. He was right, I knew that for sure. They would take us to some deserted location, shoot us, and bury us. They would kill us, just like they had done to the others. Just like they'd done to Daniela. It's possible we wouldn't be found for days, or even weeks. My mom didn't even know where I was. I was going to die in the middle of a Middle Eastern desert. We'd be reported as missing, and no one would ever find our bodies.

My thoughts wandered in that direction for another minute, unchecked. I forced myself to focus. *Get it together, Harkin! Think of something, and do it quick. Before we're all dead.*

Then I realized there was only one card left to play.

"Cardinal Montenegro," I started, eyeing the guard, who glared at me. "You're responsible for a number of deaths, including someone I cared deeply about."

Hoffman leaned forward, whispering in my ear. "This is your plan to get us out of here? Tell him he's a murderer?"

I raised my finger toward him and continued. "But I have to think there's a reason you've spent your whole life in service to the Church. You've been protecting something, a secret you believe to be true. It's a charge you've taken seriously, have you not?"

Montenegro said nothing as he stared out the window.

I cleared my throat, trying to find the words to continue. "I can only guess it must have been a task that came with its own set of…challenges. And now you are at the end of it. Your job is almost complete. Get us out of the way, the only ones who know where the tomb is, and you'll be done. Right?"

Scarlanzi grabbed my shoulder. "There is no use, son. He's already made up his…"

Salvatore saw where I was going, though, and began nodding his head. "Yes, yes, that is correct, Matthew. But there is one thing he will be missing."

"That's right," I said. "Cardinal Montenegro, you've come this far. Can you at least allow us to see the tomb together, before you kill us? Isn't there some part of you, deep down, that wants to know? You have access to the hidden tomb of Jesus Christ, and you're telling us there isn't one part of you that wants to see it for yourself?"

Montenegro continued staring out his window, hand resting on his chin.

"Consider what you are doing, brother," came Scarlanzi's voice, just above a whisper. "And our mother…think about her, Angelo."

"Enough!" he said, slamming his hand down on the seat rest and finally turning toward us. "That is enough.

198

Fine. There is no harm in going there first. The end result will be the same. If you want to see the bones of Jesus Christ for yourself before you die, fine. It does not alter your destiny."

I sighed slowly, knowing I'd bought us some more time, but not much more. We'd have to come up with something else soon.

The sky turned from pink to reddish orange, like burning embers. It wouldn't be long before it was completely dark. But when we got on one of the larger streets, we could still see the three hills in the distance. I pointed toward them.

"That's where we need to go. Toward that center mound."

In five minutes we were close to the hill. A building rose from the base of it, about halfway up.

"This is it," I said, studying the structure.

"So, just to review, you're saying the hidden tomb of Jesus Christ is in a low-rise apartment complex?" Hoffman said.

"Exactly!" Scarlanzi replied. "Or behind it, anyway. This is an old building. Probably built before they had many regulations on the protection of historically sensitive areas. It would not be the first time a significant artifact, or even tomb, was found behind a structure like this. And look in the back. The building is built against the stone hillside. This is a common practice when the builders and architects run out of room in a busy city."

"They build until they can't go any further," I said, looking at the rising hillside.

Salvatore went to the back of the truck and pulled out a long, black duffel bag. He was followed closely by the guard, who snatched the bag from him and unzipped it.

"Tools," Salvatore shrugged, waiting until the guard was satisfied the bag wasn't full of guns or grenades.

We stood on the sidewalk, staring up at the apartment building. I counted seven units across the top, each with a balcony. I studied the one in the middle. That was the one to start with, backing up to the center of the hill.

"Let's go," Montenegro said. "The sun's light is almost gone."

Pasha piped up now, as we headed for the entrance. "So we're just going to barge in on someone eating dinner, and say 'hi, how are you? Can we smash your wall in?'"

He had a good point, but I barely heard him, more concerned with how we were going to get out of this without losing our lives.

"If we have to," Scarlanzi answered.

We walked inside and headed to the central, interior hallway, finding the staircase at the end. I looked behind me at the guard as we began trudging upward. He said nothing, but waved his gun, pushing us ahead.

At the fifth level, we entered a hallway, with fourteen apartments, seven on each side.

I hoped the hallway would be full of people, anyone who might see this suspicious group and go get help. Unfortunately, it was empty.

We stopped in front of Apartment 508. Montenegro instructed his guard to go first. He raised his weapon and reached down to turn the handle. To our surprise, it was unlocked. He opened the door and we walked into a simple apartment, in the middle of renovation work.

Even worse news, I thought, facing the empty dwelling. But even in the middle of the fear for our lives, I was caught up in the reality of where we were.

Could we really be this close to the hidden tomb of Christ? Would we find it, or was this just another dead end?

"Looks like they are in the middle of fixing the place up," Hoffman muttered. "Lucky us."

I could see excitement building on Montenegro's face. He smiled. "So maybe they won't mind a hole in the wall, huh?"

Without a word, Salvatore walked to the back of the apartment, facing one large section of unpainted sheetrock. He pulled a sledgehammer out of his bag and slammed it into the wall. It cracked, plaster flying everywhere. He hit it again, and again. A gaping hole began to grow even wider. When he finally stopped hammering, we each pulled back chunks of sheetrock until most of the large wallboards were removed. Behind this was a wall of cinder blocks.

"We have to keep going." He held the sledgehammer out, breathing heavily. "Who's ready?"

Hoffman grabbed it and started swinging. The old concrete blocks couldn't hold up to his constant barrage. They crumbled on the floor.

We stepped back and waited until the dust cleared.

Behind this wall was another wall. But this one was stone, and looked like it had come out of the hillside itself.

It was ancient.

Scarlanzi stepped closer. "My friends," he said, "this is it!"

With his finger, he traced a seam across the top of the wall and back around. It formed an oblong shape. Like the front stone for a gravesite.

"It's a tomb," he said. "We've found the lost tomb of Jesus Christ."

CHAPTER 49

We were sure someone in the hallway must have heard us by now but, at the moment, no one cared. Though once I saw what Salvatore took from the duffel next, I knew it was about to get a lot louder.

"We use these in archaeological digs," he said, as he began to affix small charges in a circular pattern at the seam of the rock.

The guard watched him closely, but Montenegro signaled to allow him to continue.

"Hold on," I said. "Aren't you going to risk not only killing us, but blowing up whatever is inside this tomb?"

He smiled. "We have gotten very precise at this in the field. I know exactly what I'm doing."

Setting the charge took him several minutes but finally he looked up at us.

"Step to the back of the room, please."

We did as we were told. Holding a small detonator in his hand, he pressed the button. I winced. But there was no large explosion, just a series of pops no louder than a Fourth of July firecracker.

Stone crumbled to the ground. Salvatore brought out two long pry bars and handed me one. We moved to either side of the rock and shoved our bars as far in as they would go. I could feel that it was loose and crumbling. It wouldn't take much to dislodge it.

Salvatore looked at me.

"One…two…three!" We pulled back on the pry bars with all we had, and the stone that covered the tomb of Jesus came crashing to the ground.

Out of fascination, or sheer reverence, no one said a word. I got off of my knees and stood up. I was being summoned, as if I were being compelled to move toward the tomb. I was keenly aware of a pull within me, toward the dark hole.

The thought hit me. *If only Daniela were here.*

I didn't ask for permission from Montenegro or his guard. I simply grabbed the flashlight out of Salvatore's bag, stooped down, and took a step into the tomb before anyone could stop me.

It was dry and cool inside, with enough room for me to stand up. I flashed the light around the small enclosure, along the walls, the ceiling, the floor. A long, flat rock lay in the center of the room.

There was nothing else.

A strange thought occurred to me. I was experiencing the same thing those women who found the tomb of Jesus first felt, and then the disciples who ran along behind them.

The concrete reality that Jesus's body was not in the tomb.

There was something present, however, something invisible. A presence. It was there, as real as the breath I took. I was not alone. But there was no fear. It was quite the opposite. I had a sense of deep, profound peace flowing over me like waves. I dropped to one knee to steady myself; my head flooded with images. Pictures of my life, blazing across the canvas in my mind. My father, our trips together, my mother and the house we grew up in. I was in all of these scenes, always questioning, probing, doubting. They moved faster. Pasha and Hoffman and me, walking along an oak-lined campus path. And then images of the past few days. Margie Duncan. The assassin in the shadows. Death, pain, confusion. And then Daniela's face, staring at me across the table in the restaurant. And when we found her below her apartment, dead.

The feeling of peace transcended these images as I sat there in the cold, dark cave. Suddenly my eyes were focused on the table in front of me, the empty table where Jesus Christ had once been laid.

Words spoke to me now, coming from a long since forgotten creed I used to hear my mother say:

I believe that on the third day, he rose from the dead...

My head snapped to attention as I sensed the presence once again. This time, it was close, it was everywhere. It wrapped around me, warm and enveloping. And then, it moved past, and I could have sworn I felt a soft wind caress my face.

"*Jesus.*"

It was all I could do. It was all I could say. I whispered his name, and then closed my eyes and prayed.

I felt lost in time, but it must have only been a few seconds. When I opened my eyes and turned around, I saw the guard down on his knees, uttering something in a language I couldn't understand, tears on his face.

Pasha stood behind him, holding the guard's gun.

I raised an eyebrow.

"Apparently, he was so surprised he dropped his weapon," Pasha shrugged.

CHAPTER 50

One month later

I exited the cab and began to walk across the brick sidewalk underneath a canopy of oaks, breathing in the cool air of early morning. I pulled my overcoat tighter as I moved past green park benches and a statue of a stately gentleman. I didn't have long before I had to be back at LaGuardia for my connecting flight, but right now I needed to be here.

It was only a month ago that everything happened but sometimes it didn't seem real. I only had to remember the hours upon hours of police interrogation, though, to realize it was no fantasy. Italian, Scottish, English, and Israeli detectives all wanted a piece of Pasha, Hoffman, and me. Thankfully, Hoffman made up with his father. He forgave the massive credit card debt.

And he saw it fit to hire the best attorneys money could buy.

The Shroud of Turin was returned to the Holy Catholic Church, back in the care of the Church of Saint John the Baptist. Amazingly, minimal damage was done to it, in spite of the rough handling, and the duct tape. Scarlanzi and Salvatore were charged with its theft and were awaiting prosecution.

The existence of The Protectorate was denied by the Church, and so far no one on the outside had been able to verify the truth. Video tape doesn't lie or disappear, though, and there was enough footage of Cardinal Montenegro inside Scarlanzi's house for an arrest to be made, as well as a link to the blond, dead man at the bottom of the cliff. The Church distanced itself from Montenegro, claiming he had a very insignificant role inside the Vatican, labeling him a rogue employee operating on his own. The entire papal leadership disavowed all knowledge of The Protectorate. They dismissed the notion, likening it to other urban legends of the past.

I held a brown envelope in my hand. Reaching inside, I slid out one of the ten identical issues of Time magazine, dated for publication tomorrow.

The cover read:

Inside the Real Tomb of Jesus: Investigative reporter Matthew Harkin shares his incredible story.

Behind the title was a picture of the tomb inside the apartment in Jerusalem.

The media coverage of the tomb's discovery had been monumental. Churches were hailing it as proof of the risen Messiah. Archaeologists were lining up to study it and verify the findings. Many were calling it the discovery of the century. Naturally, some critics were panning the whole thing.

I was approached by the editor of the magazine, a woman who knew my father. They asked me to write a piece. They actually offered to pay me.

Of course, I said yes. Then, they offered me a real job. I was on assignment as an official reporter for Time magazine.

One thing I knew. My life would never be the same.

And another thing also – that somewhere, Daniela was smiling.

I hadn't spoken much about my personal encounter in the tomb, though it was all I'd been able to think about. The thought of God was becoming real to me. I am not a religious person. I am a truth-seeker. And in spite of even my own attempts to rationalize what I'd felt, I could not deny I had a brush with Him in that dark cave, when I was alone. I was even starting to talk to Him some, although I wasn't telling anyone that.

Not just yet.

I pushed the metal gate of the cemetery open and walked in. The sun broke through the trees, and there was no one here but me.

I slowly walked past the headstones, holding the crisp magazine, until I found the right one. Reaching up, I ran my finger along the cold stone, and then the letters below

BUDDY HARKIN

I missed him so much. But I also knew that life had to move on. He wanted that. I would keep going. There was a lot left to do.

The wind rustled the leaves above me, and I could almost feel his hand tousling my hair one more time. I touched my fingers to my lips and pressed them against the stone. Bending down, I stood the magazine up against the marker.

I took my time walking back to the street, realizing the heaviness I'd taken on through everything, this weight that had begun to feel almost normal, was finally lifting. My steps felt lighter; I knew I was moving forward, toward a future squarely in front of me.

And I breathed it all in deeply.

ABOUT THE AUTHOR

Jerel is captivated by stories about redemption. He is a gifted communicator and pastor with twenty years of full-time ministry experience. He holds his undergraduate degree from the University of North Carolina at Chapel Hill (go Tarheels!), and a Master of Divinity degree from Gordon-Conwell Theological Seminary. Jerel began writing fiction as a way to encourage his children's faith to come alive. He has written four books in the tween action/adventure fiction series called Jonah Stone: Son of Angels, published by Thomas Nelson - *Spirit Fighter, Fire Prophet, Shadow Chaser*, and *Truth Runner*. He lives in North Carolina with his family. *The Shroud* is his first adult fiction novel.

THE SHROUD

Made in the USA
Lexington, KY
03 April 2016